With Thoughts of Jason

Caleb A. Mertz

PublishAmerica
Baltimore

ISBN: 1-4241-1453-5
PUBLISHED BY PUBLISHAMERICA, LLLP
www.publishamerica.com
Baltimore

Printed in the United States of America

Dedicated to my best friend ever, Luis
…and to Leah, Naomi, and Carla

Chapter 1

Jason lay in his room with Snickers, his cat, listening to the festive noises coming from outside of his window. The weather was just clearing up after a severe thunderstorm, so the birds were singing madly. He stared out the window watching the dark clouds roll away, allowing the great blue sky take its place. As he stared, he thought about the secret that he had been keeping from everyone and how he was unlike any other kid in this town. They say that one in every ten teens is at least similar to him in this way. This thought comforted him; he was, however, very different from that other ten percent. He lay there getting ready to relax, completely unaware of the trials that lay ahead due to the secret he held.

The sound of the birds and the slow soft music he was playing set the mood for some relaxation. Jason lit his candles and incense with the idea of relaxation fresh in his mind. He moved the small round candle on to his exquisite display of candles and sea shells. Plastic baby's breath filled in the gaps, leading the eye in a very pleasing way. He always moved a candle or seashell to humorously make fun of his own unsettledness. To keep the from drifting outside he closed the window. As he did so his mother yelled up the stairs, asking him if he could help her with picking fresh flowers. He did not answer, instead he lay back down and summoned Snickers to do the same. Jason's eyes wandered around the room as he realized how much he liked it. It was as close to paradise as he could get.

Jason needed this time to reflect on the day he had. At school earlier that day Jason found himself walking along the corridor all alone. During this time his mind was fluttering with information the principal had just given him. He had the option of having teacher-to-student tutoring, since he was excelling in his math and science classes. These two classes were already two classes ahead of his own. Jason was amazed to hear this news, and immediately his imagination began to soar.

Walking along this corridor, Jason was thinking pleasantly about himself sitting behind a computer, receiving data from an exclusive humanoid that he himself constructed. He noticed a school newspaper on the floor and decided to pick it up. Jason, if in a good mood, would be happy to clean up after anybody. Vaguely interested, he glanced at the headlines. "Do We have What it Takes?" with a picture of the football team huddled together. "Letters to John," followed by a picture of a kid that sat two rows in front of him in philosophy. Then there on the side was the headline that altered Jason's state of being: "What's the Issue: Homosexual's Sin," followed by a picture of a grinning Seth. Seth sat right next to Jason in one of his classes. He was also assigned as his gym buddy in physical education. Jason only had long enough to read the first paragraph.

"Homosexuals that live in the big cities have been coming out and around to rural settings, infuriating the public and spreading disgust in everyone's house. So I took a poll from fellow students on what they thought about this issue. Here is what I found..."

The bell rang in the classrooms and the hallways were quickly filled with fellow students. Jason had unnoticeably stopped walking and stared at this paper. Until someone called his name, he stood there staring at this headline. He knew what he was, but there was nothing he could do about it. He began to walk again now with a noticeable new feeling in his stomach.

Walking into his first class after reading this paper, his eyes darted around to find one. There only lay one paper with it folded out to see the whole front of the paper. Jason quickly snatched it up, folded it, and placed it securely in his psychology notebook. He so desperately wanted to read it, but kept it closed so as not to raise any suspicion.

Seth, the author of "What's the Issue," walked into class with the usual crew of three other guys They took their usual seats and remained unsettled, as usual. Today, however, Jason was noticing more looks in his direction than usual, quickly followed by the ritual cackling. This spectacle unnerved Jason, so he tried his best to be attentive to yesterday's notes.

"Jason..." Seth started in a whisper loud enough for the whole class to hear, "I notice you like to talk with your hands."

The whole class broke out with laughter, and Jason turned red with embarrassment. He wasn't sure why everyone found that so funny, but he was sure it had to do with this elusive article. Seth had always made it a point to say at least once a day that Jason was gay.

"I also heard that you have a lot of girlfriends," he said, laughing at how funny it was to humiliate Jason. "Well not girlfriends, just girls that are friends."

The whole class roared with laughter once again. Jason was getting irritated, and was sick of letting everyone make fun of him.

"It's all here on the list, Jason. Why don't you take a look?" Seth pulled the paper out of his notebook and opened it for Jason to see. Looking over the list, Jason was amazed at how he really did fall into about nine of the ten categories on "How to Spot a Homosexual."

"Hmm, it's funny though, Seth..." Jason started, now finally at his breaking point. "Your mom fits just about every category here." Jason was happy with the way this came out, but maybe it came out too well. He wasn't quick enough to block Seth from rushing him.

Seth's head plowed into Jason's arm as he came in low to get the most leverage, as practiced on most football teams. Jason's desk toppled over and landed on his shoulder. A smile cracked his face, however, when he saw the bloody tooth Seth now held in his hand.

Apparently when the legs of the desk flew out, one caught him in the mouth, knocking a tooth out. Blood was oozing from his mouth now. Seth, red from pain, shot out of the classroom to the nurse's office.

Everyone sat there, at first in complete silence. The noise quickly increased, and started to make Jason sick. He pulled the paper, now on the floor, toward him so he could read this omniscient article. He was appalled at the blatant disregard of any sensitivity toward homosexuals. The underlying slander made Jason only feel sicker.

He got up and went to the bathroom to just get away from all the hustle and bustle. Usually he would have been bound to the guidance department, but not this time. No one really knew what this was like. Jason looked at the mirror at first, taking in every flaw and feature on him. He then began to not look at the mirror, but beyond the mirror. He stared into its unknown depths with dark corners for a while, before the tears began to flow.

Jason was thinking about many things all at the same time. His mind soon became foggy and unbearable. He just wanted to jump out of his body and stop this process known as thinking. When it settled that he couldn't actually do this, he threw his hands to the back of his head and gripped a handful of hair. Pulling tight, he cried. Squeezing his head between his arms, he pulled harder on his hair.

I'm gay. They hate me because I'm gay. "Hey, Jason." *What the hell do I do?* He screamed as loud as he could, "Oh God, I'm gay!" He cried now, down into his elbows. They rested now on the top of the sink.

When the teacher found him, he was as in as good a mood as usual. The bell rang for the next class, and Jason began to walk away. "Jason, what happened?" asked the philosophy teacher.

"Just a little immaturity and a lot of thinking," Jason said, quoting yesterday's notes on high school philosophy he had memorized at the beginning of class.

Chapter 2

Jason's mother closed the door to the attic after not getting a response from Jason and headed back downstairs. She was a pleasantly plump lady, as was everyone in his family, and she had dark brown hair. The wrinkles that had settled into her skin over the years were few and barely detectable. Her cheeks were always rosy and she had green eyes that were complimented by any outfit. Jason carried many of his mother's own looks. He had brown eyes instead of blue, and the nose and jaw were inherited from his father. This combination made for a very attractive young man. Jason's attractiveness was, however; obscured by his weight. Jason was chubby, not fat. This was one thing that Jason made conscious attempts to remedy. For some reason unknown he could not, however, conjure the will power needed to make this great change.

Upon her return to the back porch to get back to doing what she was doing, her youngest daughter, Melissa, sat intrigued watching her. Jason's mother was making the detergent that was so often made to wash their clothing with. Mother taught Melissa each step so that she could help her in her future. Melissa was a simple-minded girl, enthused by the smallest things and confused very easily. She loved the simple pleasures of life because they applied to her so well. With long black hair and easily tanned skin, she was a sight to see. However, just like her brother, her weight was her issue.

Jason lay in his bed so relaxed that he was on the verge of sleeping, when the tape deck suddenly stopped. The click of the button shook him from his state of relaxation. The switch from relaxed to an alarmed state at the sound of his mother's screams was instant. He clambered down the stairs as fast as his legs would carry him. His mother's screams were still heard from out front of the house. Jason slammed the door open to see his youngest sister, Melissa, lying on the side of the road. Jason's eyes immediately began swelling as his mother kneeled by her side, screaming for some one to call 9-11. Jason ran to the phone and began dialing, not even knowing what had happened to his sister.

The operator did not seem to understand the severity of this phone call. Her voice was calm and unconcerned, while he was screaming frantically. As soon as the sirens were heard Jason let her know and hung up the phone. The sound of the sirens only seemed to have increased the terror that floated in the air. He ran back to the street where Melissa lay crying, one hand on her head and the other on her left leg.

There was a crowd of people that Jason had to fight his way through to get to his sister. "…She was running across to catch the cat. It is all my fault, I yelled at her for not closing the door when he ran out and she ran after…" His mother sobbed with fear, guilt, and terror of what may come flooding her beet red skin. "It's all my fault" she continued to say as the EMTs rushed over to her, cutting their way through the crowd.

"What's happened here?" the female EMT asked, looking directly at Jason's mother.

"She got hit by a car while running after our cat!" she screamed at the EMT. Jason watched in horror as Melissa was loaded onto the stretcher. He was then able to see more damage. Her left leg looked huge and she was bleeding all over the place.

"Go on with Melissa and I will bring the other kids to the hospital," the next door neighbor said.

"Could you just watch them for a little while? Their dad'll be here shortly," she cried out of the back of the ambulance.

"Okay," the neighbor said, not being heard as the back doors of the ambulance were slammed shut and the sirens sound again. Jason ran up into his bedroom in a fit. He began crying and punching the air in distress. If he had only helped his mother as she had asked him to. He was selfish and only wanted to do as he wanted. Jason flung himself onto his bed and shoved his hands over his eyes to control the flow of tears. Thoughts continued to pound through his head as he tried to imagine what might be happening to Melissa.

Someone began knocking on his door when he jumped up. Outside was Kyle, Jason's brother, yelling, "Dad's here!"

"Okay, I'm coming!" Jason yelled back while reaching for his night coat. The trip to the hospital went so quickly with everything flooding through Jason's head, helping to keep him occupied.

Upon reaching the hospital they all climbed the stairs to Melissa's room. They made it to the intensive care unit before long. All their names were written on little badges that they each had clipped to their shirts. They continued to climb the stairs as the smell of the hospital heightened Jason's senses, making him feel dizzy. They made it to room 365, where Jason could hear his mother talking. Their steps became hurried as they were eager to see their sister.

Melissa lay in the hospital bed with her left leg up. There was a system of pulleys and weights attached to that leg. To make the children that stayed in this room more comfortable, the wallpaper was filled with little teddy bears in baby blue and a soft pink. There were wires of every sort attached to her. All of the wires led to a separate machine, which were clicking, beeping, and whizzing. The television that was set high on the wall was on, but Melissa paid no attention to it. She had just noticed her father standing there when she got excited and shrieked, "Daddy!"

"What's happened, what did the doctor say?" Jason's father asked.

"Her left femur is broken and she lost a pint of blood..." Jason's mother broke off, stepping closer to his father, turning and looking

11

directly at Melissa. Her eyes suddenly burst into tears again before she said, "They think she may never fully recover."

Jason watched his father's eyes grow wide and then begin to tear. The feeling of fear that hung in the air with the breaking of this news was thick. This lay upon everyone, except for Melissa, very heavily. The thought of this running through his head brought Jason to tears. He could not imagine seeing his little sister in a wheelchair the rest of her life.

"Why do they say that?" he asked, looking very concerned.

"Because they gave her a CAT scan and x-ray and said that her bone tissue was severely damaged, possibly beyond repair. They are just waiting for the bone specialist to come in and look over the results." At the closing of their mother's information they all worked their way over to Melissa. Jason held his little sister's hand as she looked over at him with tears in her eyes. The hurt, pain, and guilt that flooded through him the instant their eyes met was unbearable. *It's entirely my fault*, ran through his head again and again. Just then Jason's dad leaned over and gave Melissa a kiss on the forehead.

While Jason's father was bent over Melissa, three nurses burst into the room. The three nurses approached her bed and began to un-wrap the bloodstained bandages. The other nurse connected a second bag of blood. They ran around and checked the machines while Melissa eyed them wildly. The arrival of the nurses also brought about an eerie silence in the whole room. Another nurse came through the doorway holding a dark metal plate. She walked to the bottom of the bed and bent low. You could hear the metal clank against the other plates, which was quickly followed by a lurch of the leg, causing Melissa to scream. The nurse's face turned red and she raced from the room.

"We are sorry about that," the head nurse told Jason's mother. "She is new here, and I guess did not realize that we do not do things as such in the presence of the family." Upon the head nurse finishing this statement she waved for the other nurse's to follow her. As they left the room the head nurse turned and said, "I will send in the doctor."

Jason's mother mouthed "Thank you" and again turned to face Melissa. Eyes freshly red from the painful cries and skin newly tear-stained, she began to talk about what happened. They all sat and listened. All the while Jason stared at Melissa's leg, thinking about her never being able to walk again and how it would be all his fault.

Melissa, at the young age of twelve, was very enthusiastic about a lot of things. Some of the things she talked about came from thin air, but she had a unique view on several things. Jason knew that even if she heard the news that she may have to be in a wheelchair the rest of her life she would not know what that would entail. He was sure, however, that they only told his mother this possibility.

It did not seem like a long time before the doctor came through the door. "Oh! The whole family is here," he stated, looking around the bright room. He then smiled and Jason noticed a lurch in his stomach. This doctor was a young doctor, only around the age of 28. He was thin and built, with a nice coppery skin tone. He had short brown hair with blond highlights, brown eyes and pure white teeth. Jason found that he could not take his eyes off of this doctor. Realizing that he had to not make this attraction so obvious, he tried to look away, but he stared as the doctor walked over to Melissa.

"How are you doing so far?" he asked her, smiling and showing his pearly whites again. Jason took in every detail of this doctor's face that was wrinkled into a smile.

"Good," Melissa responded. "I hurt all over though," she continued, smiling back at the doctor.

"Okay, that's good," he said, obviously not paying attention to her answer and looking away from her. Opening a small bag and extracting two tubes that he snapped together, he said, "Now do you want to see a magic trick?"

"Yeah," she said. Everyone in the room stepped closer.

"Now watch this and notice how it is clear," he said, pushing something into her arm, which caused her to flinch. They all watched as the tube turned red. Melissa was confused, but everyone else suddenly felt sick. Since she was so good about this clear tube turning red with her blood, the doctor gave her a lollipop. She had realized that he took blood from her and she became very pale.

"We have to run one final test to see if she will be allergic to the antibiotics we will be putting her on," the doctor said, holding up the tube that he had taken back from Melissa's hand. "The bone specialist has made it and he reviewed the CAT scan and x-ray. He believes that we may have to do some reconstructive surgery, but she may still walk."

"We hope so…" Jason's father stated with a somewhat relaxed look on his face.

"Mrs. Lizanich, did you fill Mr. Lizanich in on what has been going on?" the doctor asked.

"Yes, I have," Jason's mother said, looking nervously over at Melissa.

"Great," the doctor replied, placing a label on the tube of blood collected from her.

Jason continued to play this scene over and over in his head all night. When the doctor came back to give them the results of the blood test, the thoughts just got worse.

"Mr. and Mrs. Lizanich, you are okay. Dr. Reckitt has a strong belief that he will be able to perform this reconstructive surgery, but it may take time. With Melissa's age, however, it should be a fast recovery and she should be on her feet in no time."

Jason watched this man breath in and out, imagining what his body may look like underneath those scrubs of his. Jason's mother and father looked at each other with hopeful glances, and thanked the doctor. Staring so hard at the doctor, Jason did not even notice him turn and look at him.

"Do you have a question for me, young man?" he asked, looking down at Jason.

Jason's eyes began to water in nervousness the second that he realized the doctor was talking to him. "Oh I was just looking at that cool pen," Jason said, now looking at a few plain blue and black pens in his pocket.

"Oh, these are nothing," he said while jamming his right hand into his pocket. "This is a cool pen," he said, handing Jason the pen. The pen was electric blue with bright purple in wild designs. It was fat at the top, and got skinny as it got closer to the tip. On the side was written the name of some medicine. "What do you think about that one?" he asked, smiling what seemed like only inches in front of Jason.

Jason stared him in the eyes, noticing how sparkling and desirable they were. His stomach was doing somersaults one after the other.

"Well?'

"Oh, it is awesome!" Jason said with a lot of enthusiasm.

"Well then you can keep it, okay?" the doctor said, now closing his mouth but keeping a smile. He then reached up and patted Jason on his shoulder and walked out of the room. Jason stood there feeling the pen in his hand and staring after the doctor for what seemed like five minutes. He then sat down and closed his eyes, unable to think of anything else except for the electric charge that he felt run through his body when the doctor touched him.

A few hours later they all packed into the car, except for Jason's mother. She decided that she was going to stay behind with Melissa. Jason did not even remember getting home or falling asleep, except for the fact that the doctor never escaped his mind.

Chapter 3

Several months had passed since Melissa's hospitalization. She was out of the hospital but was still in a cast. The skilled doctors were successful at their reconstruction of her leg. Her bone was healing miraculously, and before long she was up and trying to walk in a cast that covered both legs and her waist. She was recovering quickly from the accident, and still had weekly visits from the doctor that Jason had admired at the hospital. He always made it a point to be in the same room as the doctor while he was at their house. The doctor came to be known as Doctor John and often supplied Jason with neat pens that he kept in his room.

Jason felt the urge on one day to show the doctor the garden that he had been working on all spring, with other intentions at heart. He thought that he would be able to in some way talk to or even seduce Doctor John. With all of his hormones flowing, he would definitely be brave enough to make this attempt. After all, he had been noticing some interest on Dr. John's part. He would come over and talk to Jason nearly the entire time. He remembered to always bring Jason his pens, so of course John thought of him, even when he was not around. Not to mention Dr. John had taken a liking to just staring back at Jason when he would stare at Dr. John, thinking things only he could thankfully see.

Dr. John followed Jason into the back yard on a beautiful summer day. Jason hoped that maybe the doctor held the same attraction for him that he held for the doctor, and figured the odds were in his favor. The garden was looking good, but it needed some work. The weeds came out quickly in the fresh summer soil. Several different hues filled the garden, making a feast for the eyes. He was happy with Doctor John's reaction to the garden. When Jason and he got to the bench, Jason sat down, hoping that the doctor would sit as well. Instead John continued to stand, looking around. Eyes darting around for something to spark the conversation between John and himself, Jason sat forward in unnerved tension. Jason was finally developing a plan when John spoke without any warning.

"So what's up?" he asked.

Jason, stunned, looked up at him and saw him looking down at him with a concerned look on his face.

"Umm, nothing," Jason lied to him. This is not the way it was supposed to happen. *Now he thinks there is something wrong with me.*

"Well, you would not ask me to walk with you in the garden if you did not have a question or something for me," John said, staring down on Jason in the hot summer sun. His hands were shoved comfortably in his pockets as he adjusted his footing.

"I dunno, I do want to ask you something, but I feel really weird asking you," Jason said, feeling his face turn red with embarrassment, knowing that this would be the opportune time to be honest with John.

"Well go ahead then, you do not have to be afraid to ask anything," John said, again shifting while tugging at his pants. Jason noticed this nervous shifting and shifted himself in his seat as well.

"Anything?" Jason asked, just to be sure.

"Anything," Doctor John confirmed. Jason looked over at a bush that was just behind him. He finally worked up enough nerve to even start asking him. He looked at John in the eyes and began to ask the question, stumbling over his own words. "Well, umm...I...ummm, I don't know," Jason said, now going purple with nervousness.

"Go ahead, Jason..." John encouraged. "No matter what it is I will not tell anybody, and it will not embarrass me," he said reassuringly, looking at Jason with a kind smile on his face.

"Um, do you think my sister will ever be the same?" Jason asked, now very disappointed with himself. He could not ask John what he had wanted to ask him. His stomach was just too overactive, and Jason did not feel secure enough with himself to ask. He knew that this doctor was older than he was and he was only sixteen, so he could have no chance. All of these thoughts ran through his mind as he looked back at the doctor, only to be surprised by his reaction.

"That is not what you wanted to ask me, but yes, she will be okay," John said, looking Jason right in the eye. "Look, I catch onto things," he said, noticing the confused expression on Jason's face.

"Well no, but I did not want to ask you what I wanted to because it is an impossibility," Jason said, trying to straighten out his confused look on his face. "Granted, I wish it was a possibility."

"Well, I am sorry, but you are a little young for that...but what do I know? Well, I have to get going now, okay?" he said as he smiled at Jason and placed his hand on Jason's shoulder. "You're a good kid, don't ever change." He turned and walked past Jason, leaving him there in silence. Jason was so confused with what had just happened. Had John realized what was going on in Jason's head? Did he really know what Jason had wanted to ask him? Jason had no clue if John really knew anything about him at all.

He did not go back inside to say goodbye to John, and really didn't care to. The feeling of inferiority was so overcoming that Jason was rather angry. He stayed out in the garden and pulled some weeds to help dissipate this anger that he now held towards the doctor.

Jason stayed out in the garden for a couple more hours. As the sun prepared to make its descent, he went inside and gathered some money from his money jar. Then he cheerfully walked down Centre Street to the ice cream shop and bought a large peanut butter swirl yogurt. Wanting to lose weight, he chose yogurt instead of real ice cream.

Jason had always been a very skinny boy, but gained weight in the last five years. Having just celebrated his sixteenth birthday with his family, he didn't bother organizing a birthday party. He had only a few friends and didn't really see the need for a social life, as he dedicated his time to school and garden work. Jason felt that because he was fat, he couldn't have a lot of friends, and blamed his weight for this void.

On the way back from the ice cream shop he saw Tameera driving along with her mother, Mary. Mary beeped and waved, as did Tameera. Jason hoped that Tameera would be a new addition to his friendship circle. Tameera was a very beautiful girl, having a ballerina body and brown hair with frosted highlights. He had seen her in his lunch during school, and spoke with her every once in a while. Every time Jason saw her she was in a good mood. She always was seen with a smile, which went from ear to ear. He waved back, put a smile on his face and continued to walk home.

The days were getting longer. It had only been one week since school let out, and each day had been beautiful, warm and cloudless. The colors from the flowers and greenery shined majestically in the summer sun. Eating his yogurt, Jason sat on his lawn chair in the garden, trying to think of something to do. The garden put him in a trance-like state, no longer allowing him to think. He sat there in awe of the beauty that he created through his planting. Suddenly the garden lit up with the brilliant and vivid colors produced by the last rays of the sunset. He watched as a squirrel dodged in and out of the bushes, and a little bunny hopped along the path. He became distracted when he heard the back porch screen door open and close. He watched as his mother came out to get the laundry off of the clothes line, and soon asked for his help. Jason mumbled, but got up and went over to help.

Once inside the house Jason went on the computer. He loved talking to friends that he had made on the computer. Hours upon hours he had spent near the end of the school year, and now he talked on-line almost all night long. Sometimes he would feel guilty, knowing that he should be out doing something, like trying to lose weight, but he just stayed sitting there. Today he told everyone about what happened with John. Some of his friends told him that he knew, others said that he was probably guessing. Some thought that John might really know all about him, because of all the times John caught him staring at him. They all laughed and told him that he had been rejected. Jason played along and laughed, but really did not find it funny. The anger that had subsided since earlier in the day began to rise again.

Getting off of the computer, Jason headed into the living room, where he commenced watching a scientific program. Jason liked to learn, even in the summer time. He had aspired to be a scientist, and maybe even a physics teacher at one point in time. While watching television he heard a knocking at the door. He got up and walked over to the front door. Outside stood Jason's brother's friend Randy, looking in with his usual silly smile on his face. Randy was a strange young man who often got into hyper moods, and was constantly joking around. Randy was a tall boy, standing at about six foot, and was in good shape. He and Kyle, Jason's older brother, would play basketball a lot, even during the hot summer weather. Randy naturally had brown hair, but got blonde streaks put in it. He had his left ear pierced and had gentle river green eyes, with sparse, evenly spaced eyelashes.

"Come on in," Jason beckoned, allowing Randy to step through the door.

"Is Kyle here?" Randy asked, about to run up the old wood staircase.

"Yeah, he said he's getting ready to go fishing with you," Jason said, looking at Randy with interest flowing through his veins.

"Cool," Randy said, continuing up the stairs. He began to bang on the bathroom door, where Kyle was. "Come on Kyle, I wanna see your manhood!" Randy yelled, giggling as he said this.

"Shut the hell up, dude!" Kyle yelled back. This continued for about five minutes, when Randy came back down the stairs to the living room, he proceeded over to the couch where Jason sat. He shoved his pelvis area in Jason's face and said, "Suck it." He began thrusting and started laughing. Jason just looked at him, suddenly noticing a body part changing position. Randy went over across the room and sat down on a chair. Jason walked over to him and got on his knees in front of him.

"Okay," Jason said, making a back and forth motion in the air. Randy pushed Jason's head right into his lap. He then pushed Jason away laughing. Jason stood up laughing as well, quite confused and unsure as to what Randy's exact intent of doing that was. Kyle came down the steps and the two left to go fishing for the night. Jason was, however, very happy with Randy's joking manner. He made his way up to his room, and got all excited about what Randy had just done. Knowing that Randy was joking, Jason for some reason allowed his hopes to soar sky high.

A few agonizing days went by before Jason saw Randy again. Those few days gave Jason enough time to come up with a plan as to how he was going to make his fantasy come true. Jason figured that all he would have to do is joke around with Randy a few times, and then take some action. If Randy objected Jason could say he was sorry for taking the joke a little too far. His plan was flawless, how could it possibly go wrong?

That day, Jason asked Randy if he wanted to drive around a little while they were waiting for Kyle to get home; Randy agreed. They drove around and Jason decided to work his plan, by saying, "There's a dark alley right there, and no one would see us there." Jason's heart began pumping rapidly as Randy turned down the alley way that he had commented on. Jason thought that Randy could probably hear the pounding of his heart. He stopped on the side of the road and turned out the lights. Jason was sure that it was going to happen now, Randy's voice was so serious and Jason's intent was written all over his face. Randy must have decided that this was a bad idea, because he then laughed and pulled out of the alley.

Upon returning Jason to his house, he ran up into his room to try to understand exactly what was going on. He had to sort out his thoughts. They were flying through his mind a thousand thoughts a second. He had to think thoroughly about things before assuming anything. Needing to have the perfect plan for their next run-in, Jason lay in bed and thought long and hard for this reason. Jason was beginning to prepare for bed when someone knocked on his door. Looking at his clock he realized that it was one o'clock in the morning.

Randy and Kyle stood outside of his door laughing. Kyle said, "Jason, let us in, dude!"

Jason unlocked the door and let the two into his room. Both of them looked like they were drunk, or maybe a little more than that. He let the two of them into his room and locked the door.

They came up to Jason's room just to smoke a cigarette and wound up staying for half an hour, either talking or staring off into space. Kyle then made the motion that he was tired and was going to go downstairs to his room. Randy followed Kyle out into the hallway and to the top of the steps. Jason saw his chance quickly leaving. What a better time than this? They were both tired and Jason could get him alone in his own room! He then quickly mouthed to Randy what it was he was going to do to him. Randy then immediately turned down the stairs and informed Kyle that he was going to smoke another cigarette. Kyle said okay and closed the attic door behind him. Jason closed his bedroom door, then turned around to face Randy with a very broad smile upon his face. This was not going as planned for Jason, it was going better than he could ever have imagined!

Jason and Randy both sat on Jason's bed after their early morning escapade smoking a cigarette. Jason was rather happy, and Randy was definitely pleased. Randy was not all too willing to talk about this, as it was fresh on his mind and he was in shock of what had happened. This awkward silence allowed Jason to remember that he was going to an amusement park later that day. He looked at the clock and realized that it was only a matter of hours before his cousin got there to pick him up.

Due to Jason's overwhelming excitement over what had just happened, and what the upcoming day held for him, he could not go to sleep. Randy and he stayed up all night just talking about things, and Jason could not get that silly smile off of his face. All Jason could think about was how much he was attracted to him, and the upcoming amusement park. Jason decided to not talk about what had just happened since Randy was acting really weird about it. Hours passed by really quickly and soon Jason's aunt was there to pick him up.

Jason waved goodbye to Randy, and was tempted to run back and give him a hug. Randy offered Jason more than Jason had experienced in the longest time. The feelings that Jason now held in his heart were great, and he wanted to make Randy his boyfriend. He knew that this thought alone would be an impossibility, as Randy would never actually state that he was gay, much like Jason refused to say that about himself.

Those thoughts were out of his head when Jess, his cousin, and her friend, Danielle, began to get his attention. Jess had always been there for him, the two were really close to the point where they told each other everything. Well, almost everything, because Jason still refused to tell her that he was gay. He wasn't really sure why he was afraid, as he was almost sure that she would understand, but maybe it was the religious aspect. Because of their religion, if he told her, he might lose her forever. On the trip to the amusement park Jason didn't think much about telling her or as to why he didn't tell her. He was now mainly focusing on what rides they would go on while at the park.

As they pulled into the amusement park's parking lot, Jason stared out his window at all of the amazing thrills that waited inside those gates. He admired the tallest roller coaster on the East Coast, which was painted red and stretched high above the other rides, like a sycamore tree in a desert. There was a looping coaster that was purple and yellow, which enticed Jason to ride it as soon as he could. Then he caught sight of a roller coaster that was at the top of the hill beginning its descent. He realized that this roller coaster was an inverted coaster that hung below the tracks. It was brand new this year and he had never ridden a coaster like that before. Jason just knew that he would ride that one first.

Jason, Jess and Danielle stood in line for hours before getting on the coaster. The ride was definitely a great thrill to start the day off.

The rest of the day went by so quickly because of all the fun they were having. They all had smiles plastered on their faces and they were burnt from the scorching sun. All throughout the day Jess and Danielle were checking out a bunch of guys as they were walking. Unbeknownst to them, Jason was checking the guys out as well. He did not verbally express it to them, but merely stuck to his own thoughts. The rides were fun and the eye candy was great as the night quickly came to an end. His eyes had been treated out today, as boys walked by with their shirts off; tan muscular bodies walked past him every two seconds. Soon enough they were all walking out to the parking lot to be picked up.

The trip home seemed so much slower than the rest of the day had gone. This gave Jason plenty of time to reflect on all of the experiences of the day. Jason also felt a lot less guilty about looking at all the young men since the events that had happened earlier in the day made him feel a lot more confident. When they reached home, Jason said his good byes and went directly to his room. He did not think much about the day's events when he lay down to go to sleep. Jason was very tired at this point and his body went straight to sleep, not allowing him time to think.

Several days passed until Jason started to feel bad about himself again. He started to not look in the mirror or else he would criticize himself. He couldn't walk around with out tugging at his shirt this way and that, to try to cover up what he was hiding underneath it. He would often sit around and say that he was going to do something to lose weight. There was only one problem—he seemed to lose the drive and motivation to even try and lose some weight. He had such a low self-esteem that halted him from making this progress. He always had a smile on his face, but when he was alone, he would often put that smile on a shelf. Jason continued to pity himself. He then decided that he would go over to Rachael's house.

When he went to her house later that day he was ready to tell her about the events between Randy and himself. When Jason stopped telling her she looked very angry and upset. He had forgotten that she had been trying to get with Randy for quite some time now. She looked at him and forced a smile. "Is that all?"

There was a moment of silence between the two in which Jason really took in some of her features. Rachael had dirty blonde hair that she always put up on top of her head. She was chubby, with nice blue eyes. Being in a higher financial bracket than Jason, she often wore belly shirts, tube tops, and short shorts with expensive brand names to let everyone know her family had a little bit of money. She wasn't exactly the prettiest thing he ever saw, but he liked her as a friend— to a point.

"I'm so sorry, Rachael, I did not even mean to…" Jason said, eyes wide, realizing what he had done. "Look, I'm really sorry."

"Okay, bye then," Rachael said, still forcing a smile, but turning red with anger. Jason realized that she never expressed how angry she was, instead she flipped out. He realized how hard she was trying not to flip out on him. When she could no longer hold it in, she turned around and ran up the stairs, face in her hands. Jason just stood there feeling bad for her but also becoming a little angry because she was blaming him for what was ultimately Randy's decision. He walked around to the side door, locked it, and left without a second thought, only to be met by Randy as soon as he got home.

Jason was very surprised to see Randy there, especially since he had seen him just a few nights ago. Seeing him sitting there on the old wooden porch to Jason's house, he began to smirk. Jason could not help but to think about how Randy was always claiming to be straight, however, Jason and several other people thought very differently. Everybody figured that he was at least bi, because he liked girls, but how he dressed, talked, and looked made people think otherwise. These thoughts continued in his mind as he and Randy went upstairs. He quickly changed thought modes as Randy's intentions were made clear.

Due to this being the second little rendezvous between the two, both Randy and Jason were getting a little more involved. There was a little more motion, a little more touching, and a little more noise. Both were more comfortable because afterward they were able to comment on each other's actions. Jason did notice that Randy was not on any substance that would impair his judgment, but what had happened came very easily and quickly. Randy stayed a little longer than usual, and eventually fell asleep on Jason's bed. Jason admired him from the side of the bed and couldn't help but think that this might be going somewhere. Jason soon fell asleep on the floor next to Randy.

After a nightlong sleep full of dreams, Jason woke up refreshed. He sat up on the bed realizing that Randy wasn't there. He lit a cigarette and stared dreamily out the window. He was jerked back to reality by the sound of the attic door opening and then closing. He threw his cigarette out of the window, just as his mother came into his room. "It smells like cigarette smoke in here," she said, full of conviction.

"That is from Kyle and Randy last night," Jason said convincingly. Knowing that his mother did not want him smoking in her house, or even knew he did, he had to convince her otherwise.

"Why did Randy come down from your room early this morning?"

"I dunno, he fell asleep on my bed, so I took the floor." Jason said truthfully.

"Well isn't that such a good Christian boy," his mother said adoringly. Jason just stared at her thinking, *If you only knew*. Jason would never say something like that to his mother, so he left it at that.

She turned around stating, "I'm going to check on Melissa."

Melissa was doing really well these days, and she miraculously got a new doctor. She was going to physical therapy and she had her cast off. Her leg was really shaky, so they wanted to make sure that she did not spend all day walking around, but enough to build up her strength. She had spent about eight months in a cast so her muscles were not used to holding her up. He was so happy that his little sister was getting better, and he was able to have her help him in the garden. Whenever she worked with him outside she was happy. She especially loved watching the plants that she planted grow and become trees.

Two boring weeks passed until it was Saturday night and Randy came over once again. This time Randy didn't even care if Kyle was there or not. He came right up into Jason's room and began talking to him. Randy was complaining about girls, and Jason made some of his own suggestions, which Randy took generously.

While Jason was working with Randy he asked him for a return favor. Randy said, "No, that's disgusting." He stopped what he was doing and looked at him angered. Jason finished what he was doing (because he loved doing it), but then went straight to bed. He didn't talk to Randy at all and ignored him when he called his name. Randy then asked, "Dude, you're not gay are you?" Jason didn't reply. "Because I hate faggots." Jason still sat quiet. "Besides, this is too weird."

"What do you mean, 'it's too weird'?" Jason asked sternly.

"This whole thing is way too weird for me."

"Whatever, think what you want. Why is it then that you came back three times?" asked Jason, getting a little irritated.

"I was drunk!" Randy said while raising his voice some.

"Yeah, okay"

"What!?"

"The first time yes, but the last two times you weren't!"

"Whatever dude, I know my body more than you do."

At that statement Jason raised an eyebrow and lay down to go to sleep. He fell asleep rather quickly, considering there was someone else in the room with him.

When Jason woke up the next morning he noticed that his video camera was out, and Randy was gone. He immediately began to panic, thinking only the worst. He rewound the tape and then pressed play. He saw himself sleeping on his bed, and then the camera moved to the right and zoomed in on his Hess truck collection. He continued to rewind through the entire tape searching for something that would be really bad to have on there. When Jason was at the beginning of the tape, he fast-forwarded through it till it ended. Relieved he put down the camera and grabbed some clothes and a towel. On his way down to the shower he realized that Randy had never left. Instead he lay asleep on the bed in his brother's room, while Kyle was asleep on the floor. This scene looked a little too familiar and freaked Jason out a little.

27

When he returned to his room he lay down in front of the fan enjoying the softness of his skin while he smoked a cigarette. He knew it was going to be a bad day. As he looked into the mirror, he immediately began criticizing himself. He got into his best clothes, which consisted of baggy jeans with a tight waist and a shirt two times too big of a dark blue shade. He never wore shorts because his legs were pale and chubby. He wore massive shirts so it was harder to see his fat pockets.

As he stood in front of the mirror putting himself down more and more, his cat came running over to him, eyes ablaze with happiness. She got out a crackled meow before Jason picked her up and cuddled her. She loved it when he did this, and he knew it. He spent a few more seconds with her before he put her down on the chair. His thoughts slowly switched from Snickers to the rapidly upcoming school year. This summer went by so fast. He had barely seen his friends, as he now had more things to do around his house. He was dreading the fact that he would have to go and buy paper and folders. The only thing that he did look forward to was shopping for clothes. School would start the next week and he had paid no thought to it until now.

Instead of focusing too much on school approaching, he walked on over to Rachael's house, with a cigarette in hand as an apology. She looked to cigarettes for everything, and even accepted them as money. When he turned the corner down Rachael's alley, the wind got knocked out of him. This was soon followed by a scream, and then a hug. When Jason was able to focus his eyes he saw that it was Rachael.

"I did it!"

"Did what?" Jason asked, fixing his glasses in order to see her better.

"I umm, well you know!" she shrieked while making a symbolic movement involving her hand, tongue, and mouth.

"Really! With who?"

"Randy!"

"Cool!"

"Yeah, come on, I wanna tell you all about it," she said, practically in tears. Jason followed her back to her house and then sat listening to her story. He watched her go through a range of emotion, faces, and thoughts before she actually stopped. She then asked him about what he did with Randy. He told her about everything, which only took about fifteen minutes compared to her hour and a half lecture. She was shocked with the three times fact. No sooner than he finished his story did the doorbell ring. Rachael jumped up and went over to the door and opened it. In came Randy and Kyle. Randy saw Jason sitting there, but went right over to Rachael, paying him no mind. He began to touch her, and before long the two were heading upstairs.

Jason and Kyle were nearly done smoking cigarettes when Randy came back down the stairs, and sat down next to Kyle and lit up a cigarette. Jason went upstairs to try and find Rachael. He found her in her room crying and holding a pillow. Jason did not really want to ask, but felt obligated with being her friend and all.

"He told me that this was too weird and we couldn't do this anymore..." she said trailing off to blow her nose into a tissue. "We started doing things, and then he just stopped and said that we couldn't do this, and that... oh Jason, he has a girlfriend!" she said, now making noises as she cried.

Jason began rubbing her back, but she stood up out and ran down the stairs. He tried as hard as he could to keep up with her. When they got downstairs they saw that Randy and Kyle were leaving. Rachael ran into the kitchen, and then out of the house suddenly began throwing eggs as Randy's car. She then reached down and picked up Kyle's iced tea that he accidentally left there, and aimed it for his moon roof. Most of the iced tea made it into his car before the moon roof was shut tight. Randy then quickly peeled out of the alleyway. Rachael then turned to Jason and yelled, "Leave!"

"Why?"

"Because!"

"Because why?" Jason was asking, trying to figure out what he had done that was so bad.

"Just go!" she screamed at the top of her lungs, only inches from Jason's face.

"Alright, see ya," Jason said, getting his things together in order to begin walking home. He did not want to stay there with somebody that was yelling at him for no reason at all. He was only home a few hours when Rachael called him and said that she was out front of his house. When she arrived just a few seconds later, she had a cigarette in her hand and hair up as usual. She beckoned him out onto the porch with a smile on her face.

"Guess what?" she began.

"What?"

"Randy and your brother came back a little later, when Jacquelyn and her friend were over. Well, anyway, I told your brother that Seth gave Randy head."

Jason began to laugh right a way, because nobody liked Seth. He was another boy from their school that was so nasty, and was afraid of one thing. That one thing just happed to be of gay people.

"Yeah I know, and your brother was like 'that's nasty,' but then I told Jacquelyn and her friend, who really did," she said with an air of mystery in her voice. Jason knew that she would come up with someone else's name that would have an even bigger effect.

"Who did you say did?" Jason asked with a smile on his face, expecting a million names that could come out of her mouth.

"Who do you think?" she asked calmly, raising an eyebrow.

"Umm…Jesse? Nick? James? Cassandra?" Jason laughed, enjoying himself, thinking of Rachael's brilliant plan of embarrassing somebody so bad.

"Um, no," she said, looking rather confused with her eyebrows scrunched together.

"Well then, who?" Jason asked, still smiling ear to ear.

"Well, who else but you?" she said.

Jason felt his throat and stomach trade spaces and gasped for some breath at the shock of what had just happened. His face dropped from a smile to his mouth hanging wide open as he turned red. The last thing he ever thought she would do was betray his trust, but that's exactly what she had now done.

Chapter 4

School had begun and Jason was still in a bad mood. He had just lost what he thought to be his best friend. He was currently the talk of the town. Jason didn't even know half the people that were talking about him. He could feel the eyes of everyone boring into him as he walked through the halls at school. Everywhere he went, he watched people catch his eye and then hurry into little huddled whispers.

Jason's first class was a small class with very few people in it. This class was News Production. They would learn how to operate the camera, how to edit video clips, and how to create the streaming video that would be fed to the school. He was really sorry he signed up for this class, because it would bring him more unwanted attention. His second class wasn't any better. This class was Drivers Education; it was filled with a variety of people, including Rachael and Seth. He was not all too excited about these classes because everyone was talking about him, and he was trying to think of a way in which he could stop these rumors. Although he worried about what people were saying about him, he also thought about what people were saying about Randy. The last that Jason saw of Randy, he was in tears asking Rachael why she would say what she did to start these rumors. Jason was so sorry that this little tiny event between two people had made become like an atomic bomb exploding.

Due to Jason appearing on the TV announcements every so often, it took a while for the rumors to wear off. By the time they had, Jason had heard a million different versions. Most were bull, but only a few even came close to what had actually happened. Jason was able to hear people talk about the rumors and show no emotions to confirm or deny them. Jason was at the guidance counselor's office every once in a while with emotions high after hearing some ridiculous account of what had supposedly happened. This was all finally being put on the back burner due to the end of the semester coming up, which allowed Jason to live more freely.

Jason's social life began to sprout anew with the end of the semester rapidly coming. Now people actually began to talk to him. The people that didn't talk to him were obviously very close minded or homophobic. Jason was glad these people didn't talk to him, because if they couldn't accept him for who he was, he wouldn't want to change himself to suit them. He had lost a lot of weight due to the stress of the first semester so he was looking a lot better. He went from being 250 pounds to 200 pounds. He was really beginning to feel better when he was invited to a birthday party in Atlantic City. Jason was so excited, as this was his first birthday party in years, and he had never seen the ocean before. The party would be happening all day on the coming Saturday, and Jason could not wait.

He was really surprised at all of the good that was coming out of what had happened so long ago. Even some of the "cool" people were at least vocalizing greetings as he walked past them. This had all been so very ugly in the beginning; being taunted every day at school, hearing rumors, etc. Now, though, the tables were turning. Jason was actually making friends that liked to go bowling, clubbing, played pool, went places, and were not afraid to meet new people. The transformation was so unexpected, but thoroughly welcomed. Jason would never have imagined in a thousand years that his life would change so much.

Jason continued taking notes in Human Anatomy, but was also busy writing notes back and forth to one of his new friends. She was trying to invite Jason to a party this Saturday. He had to write several times that he already had plans to go to a birthday party with Amanda. It was Amanda's birthday party, and he knew her from working at Dunkin Donuts. Amanda knew that Jason was gay, and was happy to have only been the third one to know that he was gay. The first person he ever told was Rachael, then Elica (a friend of a long time) and then Amanda. He had just finished writing once again that he wouldn't be back at eleven, because he would be in Atlantic City, when the teacher snapped up the note. The substitute teacher was way cooler than the normal teacher, which was proven by her reading the note, smiling, and then giving the note back.

The bell rang soon thereafter and out into the hall the students sped. Jason always tried to get to lunch early so that he wouldn't be standing in line for long periods of time. When he got his food, he went over to a table and began to eat. Jason did not really know the people that sat next to him, but he really did not care, he ate his food in delight. When he was almost done eating, he glanced up at the clock and saw a friend of long past walking towards him with arms outstretched. Jason hadn't talked to Angel in years.

"Hi, Jason."

"Hey, what's up?" Jason replied, bewildered at seeing her.

"Nuthin; I just wanted to ask ya a question."

"Okay…Shoot."

"Well obviously I hear rumors and before I decide to believe them, I wanna ask the person they're about if they're true," Angel said rapidly, and then raised her eyebrows and adjusted her face as if she were apologizing for asking. Jason looked at her and smiled.

"Well tell me, my friend, what do you know?" Jason answered contentedly.

Angel whispered what she heard, which was the same everyone else had heard. Jason whispered back to her, fixing some of the askew facts.

"Oh my god!" she burst out, almost knocking the girl next to her off of her chair. "So you are!" she yelped again. She then appeared to punish herself, by slapping herself in the face and struggling to bring her voice down. "Jason, are you bi?" she asked excitedly.

"Well, I am actually leaning towards gay right now," he replied, soon followed by a grunt as Angel gave him a tight bear hug.

"I'm bisexual! Isn't that so cool! Me and you, once best friends, and now non-hetero!" Angel shrieked while trying to contain herself so that no one else could hear. The other girls sitting at the table with Jason could not hold back anymore. They all turned to see what was going on. Angel noticed this and began turning red.

"Yeah, that's pretty weird," Jason stated, staring transfixed at her.

"Well, Matt's bi," Angel told him, now calming down. "He'll be so happy when I tell him that somebody else in his class is gay," she said, now looking at the floor as if she were hatching a plan. "Okay, well, see ya," she said while giving him one last hug.

Jason sat through the rest of lunch and his other classes thinking about Matt. He was trying to decide if he liked Matt at all. Matt had dark brown hair that he would dye blonde and spike to "maximize his hair." He also had a broad forehead, deep inset eyes, his nose was rather large, and his jaw very square. He was also very hairy, and Jason was not nuts about hairy guys. Matt's over all figure was not terribly attractive, it was only his personality that attracted Jason even the slightest. Jason did, however, decide that if Matt asked him, he would go out with him.

The very next day Matt asked him out. He said yes. Little did he realize that he could never regret anything more. When the two went to lunch they wrote notes back and forth, which, he felt, was quite immature for two kids in high school. Jason tried to make this work between them, even though he did not really want to date Matt—he was just the only one around. Two days after they began going out, Matt claimed that it was over. Jason was surprised by this action, but dealt with it very easily. He was, however, a little appalled at the immaturity of the reason for why it was over. Matt claimed that it was because Jason wrote "Love, Jason" on one of the letters. (There was something that just wasn't right here, but Jason could care less.) He was quite sure that Matt was just uncomfortable with the concept of dating a guy, but he did not care.

Jason needing to vent to someone about how immature Matt was, so he went to see Elica the next day. When he got done telling her the entire story about him and Matt, she flipped out. She had met Matt before and did not like him, but now she absolutely despised him. Jason felt the need to leave Elica's apartment for his own safety, as things were flying through the air. She was searching for a picture of him so that she could curse him. He was lucky that he slipped out of her house with out any bruises, but dreaded what he had to go about doing next.

He had to go over to a girl's house, whose name was Heather, to work on a project for algebra. Matt would be there because he was in his group. Jason dragged his feet to Heather's door, but could not find the will to knock. He did not have to though, as Matt came up from behind him and knocked on the door instead. When Heather answered the door, Jason followed Matt inside.

Jason became very pissed off later in the night when Matt was flirting with him and getting very close. He really had no attraction whatsoever to him anymore. When Jason left Heather's house and the project was complete, he was in a bad mood. Jason hated that someone would take Jason's time for granted. He was really kicking himself in the butt because now Matt was acting like he was hot stuff and Jason was shit.

Exams were next week and everybody was starting to get prepared for them. Jason liked how fast the year was going now. It had started off going really slow, due to the everyday agony of the rumors and the people laughing at him, but now that the rumors had fallen the year went faster. He was actually having a good time now. They were still only halfway through the year, but it was going fast enough.

Jason still had a problem with Drivers Ed, since Rachael was in that class along with Seth. Jason talked to Rachael a little before class started but felt very uncomfortable. She still never said that she was sorry. He kind of felt bad for her because she had to sit right in front of Seth. It was still the beginning of class when Seth said something to Jason. Seth made the same motion Rachael had made before involving the use of a hand, tongue, and mouth. Jason immediately became angry and said loud enough for all to hear, "Last I heard, I think that was you having fun with that!" Several people said "Ooh!" but then the bell rang and everybody sat down. Jason was bearing a smart grin as he sat at the back of class. Seth continued to turn around and shoot daggers at Jason.

The entire period was filled with tension between the two, and then with only thirty minutes left in class, Rachael turned around to Seth for no apparent reason and yelled for him to shut up.

"Yo, chill home dog, I just be tellin it to ya straight," Seth said in a forced want-to-be gangster sort of voice.

"You ain't straight, so you can't tell anybody anything straight!" Jason yelled right off the tip of his tongue. He could not believe that: one, he thought of that so quickly, and two, that it was such a good comeback that Seth was not expecting. The substitute teacher had stopped talking and now crossed his arms and watched the drama unfold.

"Wow, somebody needs to see Jenny Craig!"

"Shut up!" Rachael screamed, now standing up and throwing her desk towards the wall.

"Wow, someone's an asshole!" a friend of Jason's said as she stood up.

"That's funny, I don't remember talking to you freak!" spat Seth. "You are a lazy fat cow," he shot at Rachael. Rachael was pacing back and forth trying to stay calm. "You're all outcasts!" Seth said, now standing up. He was breathing heavily, his eyes darting around looking for someone to challenge him. Jason's eyes met with Seth's just before Cleo, Jason's gothic friend, spoke up.

"Look everybody, I'm cool, and I make fun of people," Cleo said, making a face and contorting her body. Everybody laughed at this.

"You're all outcasts and freaks…" Seth said, still staring wildly around. "…and half of ya's need Jenny Craig."

"Umm, I remember a little boy that was, like, fat once, and his name was, like, so totally Seth, so who are you to like tell us what we need to, like, totally do?" Cleo said in a valley girl sort of way, then became very serious as she said, "Eat a dick, Seth!"

"Um yeah, I was fat and then I called Jenny Craig," Seth said mockingly. "But hey, don't go crazy now, don't go and kill a bunch of people now that you're upset," he said with a smirk coming across his face.

"Oh yeah you're so cool, and you're oh so smart," said Rachael, defending Cleo and getting closer to Seth every second.

"Does it make you happy that you are the kind of person that make people want to go home and kill themselves?" Jason said strongly, but feeling the redness enter into his face. Jason had planned that out before he opened his mouth. When the words rolled off his tongue, it did not sound as good.

"Faggot, shut up! Why don't ya..." he made the same gesture as he did earlier involving his hand, mouth, and tongue. "...some guys!"

"Last I heard..." Jason began to say.

"Whaaattt!" Rachael screamed suddenly in front of Seth. Seth was taken aback.

"I said that you stupid fool!" Rachael screamed, suddenly jamming her fist into his stomach. Seth was on the ground in a second. "I made that up!" she said, planting another fist into his shoulder. Nobody budged to stop Rachael, or to defend Seth. He had a few friends in this class, but no one did anything to stop Rachael's attack.

Jason was actually really happy that Rachael had said something because what he would have said would not have had any affect on him. Jason took Rachael's admittance of her starting the rumor as an apology. They still did not talk though, even after this "apology." Rachael realized how much she hurt Jason by doing so, but she couldn't apologize directly.

Jason still had a week to go until they were only halfway through the year, but he was really ready. He was sick and tired of the same old classes and was tired of making television appearances.

It was now the night before the trip to Atlantic City and Jason spent about an hour looking for more information as to what time everything was going to happen. When he found out what time everything was at, he ran downstairs to give his mother the needed information. Jason's face screwed up at his mother's reason as to why she couldn't take him. He then ran back up the stairs to the phone and began making additional phone calls. Jacquelyn's mother said she could pick him up and take him there. Jason thanked her, and began packing the necessary items.

"Honey, no," Jason said calmly, irritated with Snickers. She was on her about tenth attempt at climbing into the book bag Jason was packing. "You can't come with me, baby girl, but I would love for you to see the ocean just as well." Snickers uttered a little meow and lovingly looked at Jason, licking her chops. "Wish me luck," Jason said, making an affectionate face at Snickers. She looked at him with calm eyes, then blinked them. As soon as she was off of the bag, Jason lifted it and placed it on the floor next to his bed. He began to undress and soon lay down in bed trying to sleep. He finally got to sleep after hours of racing thoughts, some of which he could only sadly watch fly by, never expecting such things to ever become a reality.

Chapter 5

When the alarm went off Jason jumped out of bed and turned it off. He went back over to his bed and sat down, then pulled a cigarette out of the pack lying on the bedside table. Jason was very excited as he looked out the window. The sky was still dark blue with some cloud cover, but it was warm. Jason was literally bouncing on the bed. He decided that he wanted to listen to some techno, so he ran over to the tape deck and pressed play. When the music came, he adjusted the volume so it was just right and ran back over to his bed. He sat there Indian style near the head of his bed bouncing with excitement. Snickers jumped up onto the bed, only to quickly jump off again due to the strong bouncing. Jason was very hyper and anxious for the trip to Atlantic City to begin.

Jason tried as hard as he could to calm down when he realized he had an hour and a half until Jacquelyn's mother got there to pick him up. Jason only had to take a shower and everything would be done, but he ran to the shower and scrubbed his body vigorously, trying to hurry. Jason could not control this excitement; he had never seen the ocean, much less buildings exceeding ten stories. Jason occupied the rest of the time smoking cigarettes and listening to music.

While walking around in his garden later, he was relieved to see Jacquelyn and her mother pull up. He had everything ready for the day. He had about sixty dollars that he got from his mother that he would try to make last. They were almost at the park where they were to meet Amanda when Jason realized he needed more cigarettes. They found a twenty-four hour gas station and bought two packs. Soon enough they were at the meeting place. Jason saw a few people he knew but most he never saw before in his life.

The sun was just beginning to peek over the mountain top when they all began to board the bus. Jason noticed that Tameera was there along with Mary, her mother, and an older lady. On the way down to Atlantic City, all Jason did was look out the window and take pictures. Things seemed so much more interesting outside of his state.

Halfway to the city, as they were at a rest stop along the highway, someone sat in the seat next to him. Jason looked up and sitting next to him was Tameera. "Hi," she said smiling ear to ear, looking at him and turning a shade of pink. Tameera was a beautiful girl, with natural brown hair streaked with frosted blond highlights. She had sharp cheekbones and her earrings sparkled in the sun. Her body was that of a ballerina, her eyes were a beautiful brown, and eyelashes beautifully separated.

"Hi," Jason said back. "So what made you decide to sit by me?" Tameera was the most beautiful girl he had seen in a long time. *Beautiful girls*, he thought, *don't talk to ugly people.*

"Because I would like to get to know you," she replied still smiling, her pink cheeks turning into a delightful shade of red. Jason already had a red face from the instant he realized there was somebody sitting next to him.

"Really? Well that's a first. Nobody ever wants to get to 'know me,'" he said sheepishly.

"Well I do, is there something wrong with that?"

"Of course not," Jason replied, just now noticing a large stretch of water. "Wow, isn't that so cool?"

"Yeah, it is. So I take it you have never seen the bay before?"

"Oh honey, I've neva even seen the ocean," Jason let slip. He actually sounded like a feminine-type homosexual. Jason never viewed himself as the feminine type. He was always the more unnoticeable gay guy. Actually, guys that acted extremely flaming really annoyed him.

Tameera must not have noticed because she continued to talk. Jason suddenly realized that he was still way too hard on himself and a little too sensitive to how others perceived him.

"Aww, I feel so bad for you, but you stick with me and seeing the beach will be worth your while," she said, smiling and growing excited.

Then from the back of the bus Amanda mentioned that she was going to open some presents. Jason had turned around in interest, and was soon facing front again due to Tameera's pull.

"You do that and you're just wasting more of your life. I mean really, things that you take for granted really add up. For instance, if you live to be one hundred years old, and sleep eight hours a night, all those nights, guess how many years of your life you wind up sleeping?" Tameera asked in one big breath.

"I have no idea," Jason responded with a smile spreading across his face.

"Thirty-three years!" she shrieked and looked matter-of-factly at him before she continued. "Now imagine how much time you spend doing unproductive things."

"That's a lot of time," Jason said, truly thinking about the information he just absorbed. "But how is talking to you productive?" Jason asked all in good fun, interested to hear how she would respond.

She turned sharply, looked at him, raised her eyebrows and said, "Because there is so much you need to learn and I got the stuff to teach ya." A smile quickly spread across her face once again. "I wanna introduce you to my mother," she said, grabbing his hand and walking down the bus towards the front. "Mom, Mom! This is Jason, and Jason this is my mother…"

"Yes I saw you when you drove past me this past summer," Jason said.

"Oh yeah, wow, I only met you like a week before school let out," Tameera began explaining to him and her mother. "Well my mom's name is Mary…"

"Nice to meet you, Mary," Jason said, only reaching to shake her hand when she put her hand out for him to shake. He did this as a token of respect, as that was what his father had always taught him to do.

"…And this is Grammy Winnie," Tameera said, pointing at her grandmother palm up.

"Nice to meet you, Jason," her Grammy said while putting her hand out palm down. Jason grabbed her hand and kissed it.

"The pleasure is mine," Jason replied, as they all began to laugh. Jason looked up at Amanda just quickly enough to catch her evil glance, as they were the only ones not watching her. Jason felt bad; after all it was because of her that he was going to Atlantic City. Jason and Tameera went back to their seats and began to talk rapidly.

Before long, they were exiting the bus and walking onto a sidewalk with and entire block of demolished buildings. The hotel they needed to go to was straight in front of them and they all began to walk. Jason and Tameera had stopped talking as they looked around and about. The noises around were loud, and the people great. Jason tried to see the ocean, but was unable to. They reached the tower and walked into the lobby. This was a nice hotel; it had beautiful red cherry wood tables, crystal candelabras, and an extremely large glass, maybe even crystal, chandelier. This hotel was a lower class hotel compared to the Taj Mahal, but this was exquisite. When Amanda's father informed everyone of this fact, Jason's face became screwed up. *How can anything get nicer than this?* Jason thought as the brass staircase caught his attention.

The group took elevators up to the upper lobby, which was about three quarters of the way to the top, and which had a beautiful view. The lobby was small and unoccupied. Continuing through the door in front of them, Jason gasped. There were windows that stretched from floor to ceiling. The walls were red with a gold and blue trim, and the carpet was red as well. The furnishings of this massive dining room were super fancy. They had leather, cotton, polyester, and silk decorations. The lighting was very fashionable, and the strategically placed tables were eccentrically chic. Jason's wandering gaze was interrupted when Amanda's father said that they all had to go into the lobby and through another door. As it had turned out, they walked into a private party. The other room they walked into was very handsome and warm, which led into a pool room, arcade, and a pool. If you went into the arcade room and out the back you would end up on a roof with a warmed pool and hot tubs.

Jason ran to the edge of the roof and looked over the side to see the ocean. The ocean looked really weird to Jason, mostly because he could see so far. This large mass of water sitting there just did not seem right to him, his mind could not comprehend this. There was this massive space that was just filled with water. There were no houses, trees, hills or even mountains. The only thing that prevented you from seeing across the world at this point was the curvature of the world. All of these thoughts were running through Jason's head at a thousand miles an hour.

He realized that his enthusiasm was pitiful, but he never really saw life outside of his little town. He began thinking of the million and one things that he and Tameera could go and do. Jason enjoyed standing at the top of this building. His skin was so sensitive that he could feel the ocean's mist hitting his face. Then again, maybe he just thought he could. Tameera came up next to him and looked out over the ocean with him. When Jason turned and looked at her, her body shined in the early morning sun. She looked so beautiful standing there in her bathing suit. Jason noticed her wonderful and perfect body figure and couldn't help but wish that he were her. She then looked over at him and smiled.

"Are you gonna go into the hot tub with me and the other girls and guy?" she asked smiling.

"No, I plan on just standing here and admiring the ocean."

"Well have fun, but you should really join us," Tameera said, raising her eyebrows and beginning to walk away.

"I'll have to think about it!" Jason yelled after her, spreading a smile across his face. Jason did just as he said he was going to do.

After standing there admiring the ocean, he went over and sat down by a lady that was sitting there smoking a cigarette. "Hello," Jason said, attempting to initiate a conversation.

"Hi," the lady said in response. She was plump, with black hair tied up at the top at the back of her head. She was wearing sunglasses and a dress that looked more like a robe, which flowed freely in the fall breeze.

"Beautiful day, no?" Jason asked, once again trying to spark a conversation with this lady.

"Yes it is," she said, taking a drag from her cigarette. Following her hand he noticed that she was wearing a bunch of different necklaces, all of which had little symbols and figurines hanging from them. "We're so lucky to have a warm streak in the middle of November."

"Yeah, really, thank God because we came down today, and I had never been to the ocean before, but it is so nice out."

"Yes it is…" She began to say, before everyone began to call him in, as Amanda's parents had to make some announcements.

"Well I have to go now, but it was nice talking to you." Jason said, reaching his hand out to shake her hand. She shook his hand right back. What happened next Jason could not have anticipated. This lady's face fell, and her eyes seemed to go blank. Jason said, "Are you all right…ma'am, are you all right?" Her grip only tightened and her eyes, which had become pale, rested on his eyes.

"Have fun now. You might not get another chance, and friendships made today will last a lifetime. They may drain you, but they will be worth it." Her grip loosened and he was able to pry himself free of her. Her face went back to normal, and she walked over to the edge and threw her cigarette over, then rushed inside. Jason stood there with the creeps, knowing that he just experienced something very rare. This lady just became possessed or something right in front of him, but only when he touched her. Jason walking back to the rest of the group and began wondering if there was something wrong with him. He mentally thanked the lady that he could no longer see, and stood with everyone else.

44

"...there will be no alcoholic beverages and no use of illegal substances..." Amanda's mother was saying as Jason walked into the room.

"Mom! I really don't think anybody here is gonna do that!" Amanda said with a tone of aggravation.

"Sorry honey...Everyone; be back here at twelve-thirty for Amanda's birthday meal and cake. The meal and drinks are on us," Amanda's mother finished, and pulled a little cake out from behind her back, with happiness and enthusiasm spread across her face. In the cake was a candle with the number sixteen on it. Her mother went to give it to her, when she tripped and the cake fell and smashed on the floor. Everyone laughed except for Amanda, her father, and Jason. He felt sorry for Amanda's mother, since she seemed a little slow. Her mother was just trying to express her love for her daughter, but it got blotched, and Amanda became angry. Amanda stood up and led everybody down to the boardwalk, which made everyone quickly forget about the cake fiasco.

At the boardwalk, everyone separated into little groups. Jason initially headed towards Amanda's group before Tameera, Jacquelyn, and Cleo called him to their group. All of them, including Tameera's mother and Grammy, walked the entire boardwalk. This took a very long time because they were looking at the little shops and spending money here and there. Once they all walked the length of it two times, they stopped at an un-crowded part of the beach and ran into the water. Jason and Jacquelyn were the only two that didn't strip down to their bathing suits. They took off their shoes and walked in just enough to get their calves wet on a high wave.

Jason really got into taking pictures of the muddy water flowing in. He was initially trying to capture the moment the wave crested over. He then heard Tameera's shriek of her wanting him to take a picture. He looked out towards Tameera and was amazed at the visual effect with the water flowing around her, and the sun shining down on her in between the clouds. This effect gave an awesome silhouette against the quickly clouding sky. If he did not know any better he would have thought that she was an undine from the deep dark ocean. Jason took maybe a total of three pictures of her and then decided he would take a picture of Jacquelyn. He looked to his right, where she had been a second ago, but she wasn't there. He looked to his left and saw her walking away from a dark little corner, putting something in her purse and coughing. She walked up to him, blinked a few times with a red face, smiled and raised her eyebrows as if to say, "Hi."

Jason had been exposed to it a few times already, and he was smart enough to know what she was doing. Before in his life, he would have told someone about it, but before in his life he would also not have had friends. Jason looked at it as a balance. He said nothing but "hi" back, and continued with his picture-taking frenzy.

When everyone got bored, and a particularly nasty odor came over the beach, everyone went back to the boardwalk. There Mary and Winnie were talking to a lady dressed in black rags. She had a cart with boxes and clothing in it, which gave a major hint to Jason that she was homeless. She was enjoying a piece of pizza Mary had bought her when the kids came over. Cleo saw the pizza and ran over to the pizza shop. She came back with pizza for everyone; she even gave another piece to the homeless lady, whom they found was named Yolanda.

Cleo, Tameera, and Jacquelyn didn't eat their crust. They had offered it to Yolanda but she denied their offer. They were about to throw it away when Jason hurried up to stop them. He had come up with an idea to provide for some entertainment. This was such an obvious idea that he couldn't believe no one else thought of it. Jason took a little piece of the crust and threw it in the air at a seagull. Next thing they knew, they had ten seagulls around them, then forty. All four were enclosed in a ball of seagulls. Jacquelyn got freaked out and gently kicked her way out of the circle. Tameera was having the most fun, holding the pieces out in her hand and shrieking when a bird swiped it from her hand. They were eventually all done, and so they scared the birds away by stomping at them and screaming. Cleo was impersonating a chicken, and seagulls were just following her. That was a riot just to watch. Eventually, though, the seagulls flew away, but those few minutes were the most fun they had all day.

All four of them decided to walk on the boardwalk again to look at the attractions, stores, and boys. Jacquelyn made a few comments, helping Jason to realize that she thought he was gay. Jason really didn't care anymore, as if everyone didn't already think he was gay. Jason had just remembered to put on his visor that he had bought the night before, when he saw the most amazing specimen of a man. "Wow," Jason thought out loud. All of the girls turned to look at what Jason was looking at.

"Ask him for his number!" Jacquelyn demanded, putting a smirk across her face.

"That is not what I'm looking at..."Jason lied, "...I'm checking out his girlfriend." Jason had just watched her come around the corner, grab his muscular tanned arm, and give him a big wet one. Jason turned away. "Well looks like I don't have a chance now, do I?" Jason said, looked down and started to walk again.

"Ah, she was a ho anyway," Jacquelyn said, turning to look at Jason, smiling ear to ear. Jason wasn't sure which way to take that comment, so he left it at that. Jacquelyn was a white girl who tried to act gangster. She was plump and had black curly hair. She came from Arizona and always had stories to tell. She and her mother got along really well, almost too well. Both of them constantly complained about the girls in town, and how they talked behind everyone's back. Truth was that both of them did exactly what they complained about.

Jason was out of his Gatorade and was thirsty, so he stopped at a stand to get a can of soda. He picked it up and opened it and began to drink. He placed the fifty cents on the counter and began to walk away. "Hey! Hey, come back here!" Jason heard someone yelling. He turned around to see a man running at him. "That's a dollar fifty! I need one more dollar!" the man screamed while pointing at the fifty cents in his hand.

"Sorry, um I didn't know," Jason said while turning red and putting the dollar in his hands. Everyone started laughing at him. He told them all to shut up, and they continued walking.

Not much farther up the boardwalk, they all decided to sit down and people watch. This also gave them all a chance to calm down and relax. Sitting there, they saw people pulling up their flies, adjusting bras, groping each other, and other embarrassing things. They sat there and watched the guys going past. Jason had seen a few who looked like they were gay, but he wasn't sure. Not to mention he didn't say anything to them because he was insecure about himself. He would make comments on the passing girls to try and not seem so obvious. After every comment he would hear Jacquelyn sigh and tut. Cleo and Tameera got a few phone numbers by then, even though both were going out with someone at the time. Jason and Jacquelyn didn't, and both of them were single.

They got up from their seats and began to walk around again. Tameera and Jason went to the pier with the rides on them. They rode the Crazy Mouse and the Pirate Ship. After that their money was short for the rides. They were really tempted to spend more money, but decided not to. When they got back to the group, they saw that Grammy was walking away. They asked Mary what she was doing, and she said that she was going to gamble. Mary looked at her watch then and screwed up her face. "Mom! You can't gamble! We have to go to the birthday lunch now!"

"Oh, okay, but I still have to gamble, Mary. I am feeling a lucky streak," she said, winking at Jason. He just smiled and began to walk on with his new group of friends. They all had to get back to the hotel in five minutes, which was all the way at the other end of the boardwalk.

They rented bikes and sped most of the way to the hotel. You aren't supposed to take the bikes off of the boardwalk, but they did anyway. They reached the hotel and met up with a few of the other groups and went up the elevator. They arrived at the dining room floor and proceeded towards the dining hall. Upon arrival, each kid got a birthday hat put on his or her head. Amanda and her mother's eyes were red, and Amanda was helping her mother with the hats, a smile still on her face. Jason could only imagine what had made both of them cry.

The food and cake was very good, but the weather was getting dull. The sky was gray, the water murky, and coldness was coming over them. Several more hours of boardwalk time took up most of the evening. The groups were sitting on the steps of the Taj Mahal, waiting for Amanda's parents to come and get them. Tameera and Jason sat on a secluded step and talked about serious topics. Tameera had asked him about the Jason and Randy rumor. Jason told her that it was true.

"Wow, well that's cool," Tameera said.

"Yeah, but I am definitely trying to keep it under wraps…" Jason stated clearly. Tameera nodded her head in understanding. "…like don't even tell Colin." Colin was Tameera's boyfriend at the time, and was one of the cool kids, so Jason didn't want him to hate him as well.

"Okay, I won't say anything to anyone, not even my boyfriend," Tameera stated, a smile spreading across her face. Jason for some reason did not even question this, and instead smiled, thinking that for once in his life there was somebody there he could actually trust.

Chapter 6

Only a few more minutes passed of sitting on the steps and waiting when Amanda's parents came down from above them. "All right, listen, we have to go through the Taj, nobody go on the casino floor and stay outside of the yellow line that marks the floor. Also, do not stop and mingle," voiced Amanda's father. Everyone stood up and began to walk up the steps through the door.

Jason was distracted by the beautiful interior of the Taj Mahal. The indoor plants and everything bordered in what looked like gold were enough to get Jason's attention. Then he noticed the awesome columns, slot machines, poker tables, dice tables and the illuminated floors. Jason did not realize how long he was standing in that same spot until a casino security guard came up to them and told them to get off of the floor. They continued through to the back of the Taj. Everyone with a camera wanted to get group pictures in the back lobby, which was furnished with magnificent red leather high-backed chairs and beautiful gold-encrusted pictures. After all the pictures were taken they all hurried into a little shuttle bus that was taking them back to the big bus that would be taking them back home. The trip home was like a really long movie. They all started out laughing, and then before long some voices faded. Soon there was only a small group of girls in the back talking in raspy whispers, which kept Jason's eyes open.

He watched the muted movie for a few minutes, and made constant glances out of the window before he even started to feel tired. He had even noticed the whispers, from the girls in the back slowly die away. His eyelids were getting heavy when he heard Amanda's little brother, who was sitting in front of him, move a little. Jason looked down, and then leaned back again to try and go to sleep.

Jason's eyes had only just closed when a piercing scream penetrated his ears. He opened his eyes to see what was going on and did not have to look too far. The seat in front of him was shaking violently, and heavy breathing could be heard. He stood up as quickly as he could and looked over the back of the seat to see what was going. Amanda's brother was shaking violently and foaming from his mouth. He looked extremely pale, and his skin was beginning to acquire a bluish color. Jason watched in horror not knowing what to do, when Amanda's mother came rushing over and shoved her fingers into her son's mouth, forming a V. Before long Amanda came running to the front with a worried look in her face.

The bus driver was pulling over onto the shoulder at this point, and a couple heads were poking above their seats. Amanda's mother and father were scrambling over each other, picking up the child and splashing some water in his face. They appeared to have done this before. The sound of crying finally broke through the panicked silence, and Amanda's parents' faces relaxed. A feeling of relief fell over the entire bus. They forced their way out of the bus to get the kid in some fresh air. Jason's heart was pounding because for the first few moments he thought he would have to save this kid somehow.

How could he save somebody when he had no idea what was wrong? He still did not know exactly what was going on. Jason nudged Tameera, who was sleeping all through the commotion. She woke with a start, "What's going on?"

"Amanda's little brother just had a stroke or something," Jason retorted, a hint of fear still lingering in his voice.

"Oh yeah, he does that sometimes when he gets tired and tries to stay awake," she said, sitting up a little and looking around for Amanda's little brother.

"Oh," Jason said, still a little visibly shaken by what had happened. The bus door opened and Amanda's mom, dad, and brother came in through the door. Jason looked up in concern, as did Tameera. They just looked back and nodded at the two and sat down. One thing Jason could not watch was people in pain. It would tear him up inside and he would go into shock; he just did not know what to do in these situations.

A few minutes passed and soon Tameera was asleep again. Jason watched Amanda walk towards the back of the bus again before he finally fell to sleep. He lay, sleeping there, next to his new best friend, whom he felt a direct connection with. They bonded nearly instantly and it was like they knew each other forever. A smile spread across his face not too long after he fell asleep, the first true smile in a long time.

Jason woke with a start when the bus slowed to a stop back at the building where they had all met in the first place. Tameera simply opened her eyes and looked over at Jason. She then put a smile on her face and said, "Hello."

"Hi," Jason said back, smiling at her. She then sat up straight and stretched and made the cutest little face when she did. She looked back at him and saw that he was still looking at her and smiling.

"What?" she giggled, bringing her arms down from the long stretch.

"Nothing…" Jason laughed and turned away, lighting a cigarette as soon as he got outside of the bus. Everyone stood outside of the bus and talked about the preceding day with excitement in their tones. After about half an hour it was only Jason, Jacquelyn, Tameera, and their parents. Jacquelyn's mother had indicated that she wanted to go, so they finished up their goodbyes.

"Aww, I wish you didn't have to go," Tameera said to Jason, holding both of his hands and pulling him closer to her.

"I know, but we could hang out tomorrow," he said with a questioning voice to see if she agreed.

"Yeah, we can," she said thinking quickly, "...first thing in the morning. Okay?" she said, looking at Jason anxiously.

"Definitely," Jason confirmed and he got into the car. "Give me your number so that I can call you when I wake up."

"Okay, but don't call before eleven-thirty, cuz I probably will not be awake."

"Okay," Jason said laughing and got into the car. Tameera got into her mother's car as well, and they both drove off. At the light they all went different ways. Jason was uneventfully dropped off at his house later that evening after going for coffee with Jacquelyn.

The next morning Jason was up by ten o'clock in the morning, so he knew that he had at least an hour and a half to wait to call Tameera. He was surprised when he received a phone call not more than fifteen minutes later. It was Tameera asking him how to get to his house. Jason went to Tameera's house to hang out for a little while. Colin was there and the two seemed to not be able to keep their hands off of each other. Jason didn't say anything, even though it did make him uncomfortable. They calmed down after they disappeared for ten minutes and left Jason talking to Mary, Tameera's mother.

Tameera was so funny and was a lot of fun to hang around with. She seemed to be very simpleminded, though she really wasn't, but she would laugh at almost anything. Jason felt really comfortable at her house and around her parents.

Tameera had a way of letting Jason know that he was appreciated. When Colin left, Jason and Tameera spent hours out on her front porch talking.

"So how did we never meet before, like earlier in the school year?" Tameera asked.

"I dunno," Jason responded, "but I wish we had."

"Yeah really, we just like bonded so easily."

"Yeah, but I was so nervous when you first sat right next to me on the bus."

"I know, your face turned all red," Tameera said giggeling, "but then you started to relax and I could tell you were gay," she said, still laughing.

"Why didn't you say anything?" Jason asked, looking bewildered as he did not remember a reaction of any sort comng from her.

"I wasn't going to let my first question be, 'Are you gay?'"

"True, because I would have felt really uncomfortable."

"I know, I would too, shoot!" Tameera said laughing. "So why don't you tell anybody about it?" she asked in honest interest.

Jason just looked at her. He then looked down and began to pick at the skin around his fingernails. "Because then my family would find out and since we're Christians, they would disown me and treat me like crap," Jason said, still looking down at his fingers.

"But why would they do that?"

"Because they only believe what the Bible says, and don't look at me like I'm human. Instead, if you're gay, you've been 'possessed' by the devil."

"Oh," was all that Tameera could say. They got off of this subject and ventured into many other topics of interest. This probing of Tameera's did really get Jason thinking about why he held it in and didn't tell anybody.

After spending a few hours at Tameera's house, her mother took him home. When Jason got home, his brother Kyle began to interrogate him. When Jason told him that he was hanging out with Tameera, he looked at him with disbelief. "Dude, I wouldn't get involved with that girl. She's a liar and she will try to ruin your life, oh yeah, and her mom is into that black magic crap," he said in his usual deep, slow voice while raising his eyebrows.

"Whatever dude, don't tell me who can and can't be my friend," Jason said, getting upset that Kyle was saying this to him. "And besides, I don't believe any rumor until I know the truth for sure," Jason stated as a final word and went upstairs to his room. Jason couldn't wait to see Tameera the next day and talk to her at school, but in the meantime he would be up in his room.

Jason opened the door to his room and was greeted with a crackled meow from Snickers. Snickers was starting to grow a little more, but she wasn't still tiny compared to the other two cats in the house. Upon entering his room, he looked at his book bag, which reminded him that he had some studying for exams to do. He sat down on his bed with a plop and pulled his book bag onto the bed. Snickers came running up to the bed and ran right into Jason's lap. Jason let her stay there at that time but as soon as his books were out, she had to move. Due to Jason's new outlook on life, which had developed over the last week, especially over the weekend, he despised having to do homework.

Jason's first exam was easy, along with his second one. His third and fourth exams were a little more difficult, since they were for his Human Anatomy and Spanish classes. Jason did well on every exam, except Spanish. He knew he would have a hard time, as he dedicated a lot of time to studying anatomy. When Jason returned home after taking his exams, he sat down on the porch, lit up a cigarette and thought about a few of his answers. As soon as Jason was done with his cigarette, he flicked it over the banister and stood up. He stretched out a little, relieved that his exams were over, and turned toward the door. He stepped foot inside of his house with plans of calling Tameera, when he heard someone yell "Hey."

Jason, being alarmed, turned around to find out where it came from. What Jason was looking for stood right in front of him. The only reaction Jason could muster was a screwed up face and a gesture for the much unexpected visitor to come inside.

Chapter 7

Jason and his friend sat on his bed staring at each other for what felt like a very long time. Adrian was Jason's first ever boyfriend. They had gone out when he was just fourteen, but it did not last long at all. It did not last long because of the situation that Jason was in, as he was away from his family at an institution. Adrian was a young white boy with some Asian influence, but not much. He had dark brown hair, eyes that slanted very slightly, a gently curved nose, and he had the figure of a stick. Sitting there smoking cigarettes, Jason's head was filling with questions but he wouldn't voice them because he was lost for words.

"Okay, kinda awkward, I guess I should have called before I came, huh?" Adrian said, looking like he sincerely felt bad.

"Umm sure…no! This is fine. I just never expected for you to ever come here just to see me," Jason said, still surprised that Adrian was sitting right in front of him.

"Well that, and to turn some 'straight' guys gay," Adrian said smiling and uttering the same old "tut" kind of laugh. This did, however, seem to be Adrian's rational. He felt he could do this because he was able to seduce older men before, specifically his mother's boyfriends. "Let's go and walk around town, shall we?" Adrian then suggested.

"Okay," Jason said, beginning to smile. He figured that instead of continuing to act shocked he would just enjoy it while it last. The two put out their cigarettes and got up to leave. Before Adrian left the room, he squatted down to Snickers's eye level and said goodbye to his "little girl." Jason laughed and so did Adrian as they left his room.

Jason realized that he wasn't going to be able to hide this from his mother, but he also knew that there was nothing she could really do. He was worried because he had recently told his mother that he thought he was gay. When he told her this she said that she knew all along, but he should really go to church. This is how Jason knew how his family would react. He let Tameera know what would happen, but for some reason he didn't tell her that he already had once. Life was never the same. His mother forced him to eat off of paper plates and use plastic utensils and Styrofoam cups. Then she always made snide comments whenever he talked to another guy. He was really happy that he did not tell her about Randy, because she already suspected something and often asked him about him.

Coming out was one of the hardest, and yet one of the worst things that he had ever done. He did not come out to too many people at school, but he came out to his mother and sisters. He still refused to tell his brother the truth, even though he kind of caught on. The stress that was piled on as a result of his coming out was more than he really wanted to handle. He was constantly looking for a way to get out of this problem that he was in, to make his mother believe that he was really straight. All of these thoughts ran through his head as the two boys walked out of the front door and proceeded down Centre Street.

Jason decided to show Adrian around and began with the "witch" shop that was cleverly disguised as a craft shop. Adrian took a fascination in the objects inside of this store, which led Jason to believe that he was Wiccan. The boys spent about half an hour in this lady's store, which resulted in the purchase of a pentacle necklace. Jason wasn't a church-going Christian, but he preferred not to mess around with things of a supposed devilish nature.

Upon leaving this store, Adrian already had the pentacle around his neck and they proceeded to the massage center. Jason was happy to be walking around today, as it was a beautiful day. The air was crisp and clean, the sun was warming, and the midday soil was fragrant in the air. At the massage center the two looked at the prices and met the lady who did the massages. Adrian wanted a massage but didn't have enough money. When they left the place, Jason promised to give him a massage. Adrian stopped dead in his tracks, looked at Jason with a smile on his face, and continued to walk. They went to the floral shop where they stood and read all of the funny cards.

They continued on their survey of the town and stopped at every store along the line. The two were having a good old time walking and talking along the old streets of this old town. They ate at the Garden Café, which was owned by Jason's friend's mother. While at the café, the two were able to talk and catch up on some lost time. The boys were successful at wrapping up three years into two hours worth of constant babbling back and forth. Jason told Adrian about Matt, and how hard it has been living in this little town. He also told him about Randy, and how much fun he had with him. He also mentioned his friends, why he chose them, and the personality traits he liked about them.

Adrian had a much more interesting story than Jason could ever have. Adrian lived right outside of the city and had plenty of access to pretty much whatever he wanted. Adrian was, however, very poor. He was a single child, and his mother spent all of her money on cigarettes, alcohol, and fast food. Adrian was happy about the food, but could never get what he wanted unless he stole it. He was only able to come and visit Jason because his best friend lent him a hundred and fifty dollars. He just recently got a job and promised to pay her back. Adrian was pretty used to stealing things, and Jason knew to keep an extra eye on him or else he may wind up missing something. Adrian came off as self-centered and arrogant, but Jason, having had the support group with him, knew he wasn't. Adrian's mother would often get drunk and order him around, and then she would slap him and call him a faggot. She would kick him and throw empty bottles at him for no good reason. Therefore, when Adrian was outside of his house, he exalted himself above everyone else to make himself feel better. He realized he wasn't better than everyone else, but liked for people to believe so.

Adrian's story of the past three years was filled with arrests, alcohol abuse, marijuana use, sex, revenge, and straight guys. Adrian was arrested several times for stealing cigarettes from gas stations. Most of Adrian's more recent boyfriends were older, and they always had alcohol. Naturally, Adrian being the rebel he was, had to get drunk every time there was alcohol around. This led to about two arrests as well. He also got really involved with marijuana, and he described the "awesome euphoria" that you go into when smoking it. He even said that if you can't get sleep, just fire up a blunt or pack a bowl and you'd be feeling pretty good.

Adrian told Jason a lot of stories about his sex life. He even went so far as to say that while he was doing the dirty with this one guy he screamed Jason's name. Jason could do nothing but laugh at this statement. He found it hilarious, because Jason and Adrian never did anything with each other. He knew that Adrian was known for being a charmer. Adrian sought some heavy-duty revenge on an ex that he found to be cheating on him. Then, of course, you have Adrian talking about straight guys and trying to turn them gay, as if it were his life's mission.

When Adrian was done explaining everything about his last three years, Jason was still waiting for more. "And...?" Jason asked Adrian encouragingly.

"And what?" Adrian asked as a smile reappeared in the corners of his mouth.

"Well...then what?" Jason asked, convinced there was more to his story that he was just not saying.

"That's it...Oh yeah, and I think about you every night," Adrian said, looking directly into Jason's eyes.

"Get a life." Jason smirked, shrugging off Adrian's charm, even though it did work a little bit. The two boys got up and walked over to the gas station to pick up some cigarettes.

On the way back to Jason's house from the gas station, he saw Tameera and Mary. They pulled over a little ahead and motioned for them to come over. Thirty seconds later Adrian and Jason were crawling into the Range Rover. "So, who are you?" Tameera asked, looking back at Adrian.

"The devil, why?" Adrian asked, putting a smile on his face. Tameera looked at Jason and began to laugh.

"No really, what's your name?"

"Beelzebub"

"Andrew, Steve, Alex, John..."

"Lucifer."

"Larry, Owen, Jacob, Jeff..."

"Belial."

"What?"

"Belial, he's a demon who is deceptively handsome and lures young men into doing shameful things." Adrian said that latter, "shameful things," like an old lady at church would say it. Once again Tameera looked at Jason and laughed. Finally, however, she had an inch of understanding, as Jason had told her about Adrian in the past. Tameera just stared at him dumbstruck and slowly began to smile.

Jason looked at her, smiled, and then said, "His name is Adrian." Tameera made eye contact with him right away, her eyes open wide.

"Wait, your Jason's first boyfriend?" she asked, now looking as though she was hit in the face with understanding.

"I guess," Adrian said, looking a little confused, but then smirking in Jason's direction. "So you talk about me to your friends?"

"Only in a good way," Jason confirmed, smiling broader than ever. Adrian just looked at him with smile that did not fade away.

They pulled into Tameera's driveway and quickly scrambled out of the car. The three went right to Tameera's room where they all began to talk avidly. Tameera eventually asked Adrian if he smoked, when he said yes, she got out one of her favorite toys. Adrian admired this device that was made of brass and had three tubes connected to it for three people to enjoy. Tameera and Adrian both demanded Jason sit there and hit the hookah, but he refused.

Half an hour later, Adrian was lying on Jason, next to Tameera. They were all sitting on her bed, stoned and drunk. Jason felt pretty good and brave. He felt like he hadn't a care in the world, and if he did he forgot what it was. He had fallen victim to peer pressure and became one with the hookah. He felt like life was perfect now, holding another guy who he could have feelings for, next to a really good friend, and not having a care in the world. Only to make Jason's world even more perfect, Adrian turned around and gave him a kiss on the lips. Jason liked this kiss, so he turned Adrian's head again and began making out with him.

This didn't last too long since Tameera stopped it as soon as she saw what was going on. They all sat and chatted while eating potato chips and drinking soda. Jason usually hated potato chips, but they tasted really good at the time and he felt like he would never be able to eat enough.

Within a matter of minutes all three were laughing up a storm. Mary stepped foot into the smokey room, moaned an "Oh God" and turned around, closing the door. All three stared at the door and then broke out in laughter. Only a minute or two passed before Grammy came running in. She leaned over the side of the bed, picking up a tube from the hookah, and inhaled deeply. She then quickly got up and left the room without a word. They all exchanged glances and began to laugh again.

After it was dark and a few hours had passed since they first made the trip to Tameera's house, Jason remembered that he had school the next day. Mary came into the room and asked if the boys were ready to go home, at which point they stood up and prepared to go. Mary had already backed out the car and was beeping before the boys got out to the car. The drive was quiet.

They got back to Jason's house and hurried up into his room. "Now tell me...why do you have a suitcase?" Jason asked Adrian. This was followed by five minutes of laughter, so that their stomachs burned.

"So that I have a change of clothes for the week," Adrian said, beginning to laugh. Jason's eyes widened in both joy and fear at his surprising answer. He would love for him to stay a week, but had a hard time imagining how his mother would take that. "No, just overnight, and then I have to go home."

"Oh okay, so you're leaving early tomorrow morning?" Jason asked.

"No, I'm leaving late tomorrow. I have to go to school to see some of these people and see what I can do, right? Now how about that back massage you promised me?" Adrian said, stripping down to his boxers and lying out on Jason's bed. Jason did not hesitate looking at Adrian's firm tan body, and wanted to keep him there forever. When Adrian began snoring, Jason bent over him and looked at him with caring eyes. Jason had never thought he would ever see him again, and now here he was in his bed. Jason felt purely happy, and so he lay down behind Adrian and cuddled him close.

School was interesting the next day with Adrian attending. He still had the same classes, but everything was just a little different that day. Accommodations were made so that Adrian could sit right next to Jason in every class. News production was awesome, as Mr. Prize let Adrian be a lead anchor with Jason. He then made a copy of the tape for Adrian to take home. Everyone in this class was really open to him, and forced Jason to question the sexuality of this one kid that seemed very keen on having Adrian's attention every other minute.

In Drivers Ed, Adrian wanted to be the center of attention and was pretty free to, as this class was mainly girls. Adrian spent a lot of time cracking jokes, really making the class enjoyable. That was, until Seth came in late for class. Jason quickly pulled Adrian into a conversation about Seth and how he was.

"Watch this…Oh and don't associate with me, I will meet you at your locker, okay?

"Why shouldn't I associate with you?" Jason asked, becoming a little irritated at this request.

"Because you have to see him every day, I don't," he explained, touching Jason's hand and walking over to a seat closer to Seth. Jason was a little worried for him, but watched his every move. He tapped the girl's shoulder in front of him, and they soon switched places.

"Jason, what do you think?" asked the teacher.

"Umm..."

"What the hell is your problem?" Seth yelled at Adrian as he stood up quickly.

"Oh come on, sit down, I just want to give you a massage," Adrian said, looking at him with puppy dog eyes.

"Seth, sit down!" the teacher roared, pointing at Seth's chair.

"Hell no, not by that faggot," Seth said.

"Ooooo!" Adrian shrieked as if Seth were flattering him.

"See! He's a freak!" Seth shouted, his face cringing with disgust.

"Oh, come on over here, and sit down," Adrian voiced, crossing his legs and resting his hands on top, while looking at him from the tops of his eyes. Adrian then decided to stand up and walk over to Seth. Seth drew back and went to punch him. The teacher's eyes grew wide, as Seth put all of his weight into his punch. Adrian's hands moved so fast, it was amazing. He blocked Seth's punch, and in one quick movement, had him on the ground restrained. He was then able to tell him to be a little more open to people; Adrian said everything Jason had ever wanted to say to Seth.

The teacher gave both of them an after-school detention and Seth received a Saturday. He then sent Seth up to the nurse's office for his bloody nose. The force of his punch and Adrian's push when he hit the floor caused this bloody mess. The class was over soon, and Jason went straight to his locker. Adrian was not far behind. "Did you like that?" he asked sincerely.

"Yeah, but now I have to stay after as well," Jason responded, looking at Adrian in contempt.

"So do something to actually deserve yourself a detention," Adrian demanded, almost getting on Jason's nerves yet holding a very good point. Next class was Human Anatomy. Adrian wanted to be late for this class, but Jason did not want to be. Jason practically dragged Adrian to class and got inside just before the bell rang. The teacher smiled and gave Adrian a warm welcome to the class. Just then, the whole class began to applaud for him, because they had all heard of what he had done. Adrian, not trying to be humble at all, stood up and bowed to the entire class. Today the class was dissecting a sheep's brain to get a better look at the human brain. Adrian was fascinated and walked around to everybody looking at their brains. He especially liked this one kid who had a model-like figure, along with perfect hair and electric blue eyes.

"And wow does he know how to dress!" Adrian said, really amazed and glancing over his way. "Okay, I have to check up on him again," Adrian said as he stood up to make his way over to his table.

Class went by really quick and it was time to go to lunch. Adrian couldn't wait to go to lunch, because he knew there would be more people there to look at. They both got their lunches and quickly went over to the lunch table. There both of them ate their food and had a nice little conversation about the guys that surrounded them. Jason pointed out the guys that he liked, and Adrian would then voice his opinion. He wasn't exactly sure what made him think a guy to be hot or not, but he knew what helped them along. He liked a guy who was built not to skinny, but not fat. He also liked them smooth with awesome eyes, especially blue or green. Blonde hair or brown hair was just another plus that a guy could have for him.

The criticism of other guys continued all through lunch, and then they had to go to fourth block. Jason was originally going to be late for Spanish, but he then realized that they couldn't punish Adrian, because he wasn't a student. Jason went to Spanish class on time because he really did not want a detention. The class was buzzing with excitement about what Adrian had done. The teacher stood up at her podium, hushing the class to silence.

"I hadn't planned on being here today, so I don't have anything planned." She paused, waiting for cheers of excitement, none came. "Um, if everyone could complete this crossword and hand it in, that would be great. Then you have the rest of the period to yourself."

Upon her finishing her statement, the class uttered a "yes," and began to work. Jason got done rather quickly and turned it in. This class was the most boring, so Jason wanted to leave as soon as possible.

"Um, I need to leave so that I can take him to the bus stop," Jason said to the teacher. "I forgot the pink slip in my locker," Jason lied. "So can I just have a pass?"

"Sure, here you go," she said grabbing a piece of paper and looking over at the clock. It was nice to get out forty-five minutes earlier than everyone else in the school. No one was in the halls, and nobody was walking home. It was quite cold out today and the two walked home, hunched up in their jackets. Upon reaching Jason's home, Adrian insisted that he take a shower. Jason gave him a towel and watched him undress. Jason turned around and shut the bathroom door, heart pounding a hundred beats per second. When Jason locked the door, Adrian asked him what he was doing.

"What do you think?" Jason said, smiling ear to ear. Adrian smiled wide as well.

"Are you going to rape me?" Adrian asked, still smiling.

"Rape you? It isn't rape if you want to."

"Well number one, I never said that I wanted to do anything with you, and I am in a committed relationship," he said still smiling.

"Well do you want me to then?" Jason asked promptly.

"I wouldn't care…but I have a boyfriend, so I have to care, don't I?" Adrian said matter-of-factly.

"Okay, well I am sorry," Jason said, wanting to cry. He closed the curtain to the shower and got up to leave the room.

"Hey! I don't want that closed," Adrian said, opening the curtain again and looking at Jason. "You can jerk off, I wouldn't care."

"I don't want to jerk off, I want the real deal!" Jason said, feeling the lump in his throat forming. Then he walked out of the bathroom and closed the door behind him. He ran up into his room and began to cry into his pillow. All of his hopes were gone; all of these signals must have been false. Why didn't Adrian tell him this originally? Jason remembered thinking that there was more to Adrian's story; that must have been it. He had a boyfriend, which is why he didn't want to do anything. How could Jason be so foolish? He also thought about the kissing and what that meant. Obviously everything meant nothing to Adrian, but it meant the world to Jason. Jason was sixteen and had yet to have a relationship that meant anything. Randy did not count.

All of these thoughts raced through his head, and before he knew it he was asleep.

Chapter 8

Jason woke up around three o'clock and scrambled to get out of bed. He ran to his door and saw that it wasn't shut right. "Oh God!" Jason said, concerned. He checked all the rooms in the attic, and then ran downstairs. He knocked on the bathroom door, thinking that maybe Adrian was still in there, but was disappointed to hear his sister scream that she was in there. Jason's eyes opened wide as he then sped downstairs and out the front door. He looked up and down Centre Street, but saw no one. He then ducked back inside and ran around his house, checking every room for Adrian. When he couldn't find him anywhere, he went upstairs into his room and shut the door. He looked over at his coffee table and saw a note sitting on top of it.

Dear Jason,

I'm so sorry I toyed around with you like that. I didn't realize that you would be so sensitive. I was joking around about the whole thing, but I feel really bad. I don't have a boyfriend and I wanted a shower because I wanted to be clean for you so we could hump like bunnies. But I left because I feel really bad for being so mean to you. I will call

you when I get home. Well, the cab is here so I better go; it's about 2:50.
    Love ya always,
    Adrian
    P.S. You are really cute when you're sleeping. Bye.

Jason didn't know how to react. He felt terrible, and so frustrated. He was angry with himself that he would overreact like that. Now he began to think about what he should have done while Adrian was still there. He then beat himself up over falling asleep. He threw himself on the bed, extremely upset over the situation, almost to the point of tears. He felt so stupid and like a complete jerk. He couldn't do anything but think about what he had done. Later that night, when he finally tried to sleep, all he could do was dream about Adrian and him together, and what could have happened. He was even more depressed because Adrian never called him to tell him he got home safely.

School seemed like it didn't even matter anymore. Jason spent the entire winter mainly depressed and trying to get in touch with Adrian. He was only able to get through this depression by telling himself that Adrian was a liar, and that he never would have actually done what he said in the letter. He had to also repeat over and over how much of a charmer he knew Adrian to be. Eventually, over time the thoughts of Adrian slipped into the few far and in between. When he would think of him, however, it would be followed by a day or two of depression, as he still had not spoken to him since the day he flipped out in the shower.

Jason really did not have much time to focus on Adrian following Christmas that year. The upcoming weeks contained more than Jason could ever imagine.

It was really cold outside, and the snow that was lying on the ground showed no signs of melting. The promising warmth of the gas station forced him into more hurried steps. Peering inside he noticed that his friend Stitla was working, so he walked to the doors with a smile across his face. Stitla was a young lady of twenty-one who had a round body and short brown hair that was dyed blonde. Her mouth exaggerated its muscle movements on the one side, which gave her mouth a slanted look. Stitla's eyebrows were very light and thin, giving them the appearance of not even being there. Through that all she wasn't hard to look at. "Hi, Stitla," Jason announced.

"Hi Jason, how are you?" Stitla asked, smiling more broadly each second.

"Good...good, you?" Jason retorted, heading to the back of the store to get some hot chocolate to warm his insides.

"Good, any luck with getting in touch with Adrian?" she asked, now moving around the counter so that she would not have to scream to the back.

"No, he's a jerk anyway," Jason said trying to cover his true feelings on this matter. Just then the door opened and in stepped a young man. Jason recognized him as an acquaintance named Larry. "Hey Larry," Jason said, as Stitla put her head down and quickly walked towards the cash register to wait on him.

"Oh, hey dude! What is up, man?!" Larry said, holding his hand up to give Jason a hand shake. Smiling broadly, his little beady eyes caught all the light in the store and directed them in all directions. He then placed one hand on his perfectly shaped and groomed goatee.

"Nothing really, same old, same old."

"Ah, I hear ya, man," Larry said, forcing his hands in his pockets to pay for the cigarettes he was there to buy. "Dude I have to talk to you then..." Larry said, then turning to Stitla, "a pack of Camels please."

"About what?" Jason asked, a little confused and worried at the same time. Larry did not know that Jason was gay, and he wanted to keep it that way. Being a serious Christian, he would never understand what it meant to be gay.

"You'll see..." Larry said, leaving Jason in an undeserved state of suspension. The two walked out of the building and went to Larry's Bronco. Jason took a step out into the crispy cold evening and crossed his arms tightly about him. Larry's car warmed up rather fast, and before long Jason was almost too hot.

"God wants you to come back to him. You have been slacking and he doesn't like that. In fact, you did something just a little while back that he was really ashamed of."

Jason drew in a deep breath of guilt. It was not often that he spoke of God and Jesus or anything having to do with religion. Jason knew what he was talking about, but challenged it anyway.

"Something just a little while back?" Jason reiterated, pushing his eyebrows together in question.

"Hey man, we're talking about God here, he knows all. What the big man says always, and I mean always, goes," Larry said, looking at Jason like he knew something Jason didn't.

"I haven't done anything that would be that bad for God to be ashamed of," Jason said now starting to get a little irritated. Jason knew that he was probably just guessing. Who doesn't go through a day without doing something they shouldn't have? If Larry, by some stretch of the imagination, was actually speaking with God, then Jason knew it was about smoking pot or being gay.

"Well come on, we're gonna go over to Pop's house."

"Pop's?"

"Yeah, Pops, you know that guy from your church?" Larry said, trying to refresh Jason's memory. Since it had been so long since Jason set foot in the church, he could not remember anybody. Pulling up to the house, Jason quickly began to survey the house. The street full of different colored row homes was nicely kept, except for the house on the corner. This house had Christmas decorations hanging that were dilapidated, motorcycles, radios, refrigerators and air conditioners. Larry led Jason to the front door, knocked a few times and then walked right in. As soon as he set foot inside of the house he was smacked with a terrible stench. The smell of cat urine, stale cigarettes and death greeted his nose with a strong and potent punch.

After the initial smell of this house, Jason was not surprised to see a box sitting there, litter strewn about, and cigarette butts just lying everywhere. When Jason turned the corner, there lay "Pops" cuddled next to his halogen heater.

"Oh, Larry, you're here good, good, who did you bring with

you?" Pops asked, looking up to see who walked through his front door. Jason stood there looking around at the interior of the row home. The living room was piled with computers, radios, video cameras, recording boards and so on. All of these pieces of equipment were taken apart and strewn all about the living room, piling up around the walls.

"Hey kid, how are ya?" Pop's asked him.

"Good, and how about you?" Jason replied respectfully.

"Good…hey is your brother Kyle?" he asked, shaking a bony finger at him.

"Yeah, that's my brother," Jason responded, smile on his face, still being polite but wanting to leave immediately.

"Have a seat guys," Pops said, opening his hands to point at the floor. It was very easy to see that his man really needed somebody to talk to. Jason did not really want to sit down, but was forced to as Larry became quite comfy on the floor. Jason, not wanting to be rude, followed suit.

He quickly searched for a way to break the silence, Jason asked about Pop's wife.

Not until after he asked this question did he figure out that she had died last month. Pops went into a very dramatic story about how good the lord was to them and then how he punished her with cancer because she didn't tithe. It was a very twisted story around God, his wife, and life's virtues. Jason personally did not agree with half of this story and this old guy's take on life. It was truly a sad story, and Jason felt bad, but for some reason he didn't feel bad for Pops.

At the end of his long speech he bowed his head and began to speak out loud, apparently to God. Jason couldn't understand what he was saying, and so he leaned in. He kept leaning closer and closer when the sudden boom of laughter from Pops caused him to jump back.

"Kid, God told me to tell you to not think that I'm crazy, because I'm not."

Jason sat back, realizing for sure that Pops was praying and laughed inside because he didn't for one second assume that Pops was crazy. Then Jason was surprised by his next comment.

"God is telling me that you're pushing him away because you're having some sort of internal conflict," Pops said, looking at Jason. Pops then looked up at the ceiling and began to utter inaudible words. "Oh, wow a very great internal conflict, and so you're pushing away from God, because you don't think he loves you anymore." He then chuckled a little bit and said, "But Jason, God loves every single one of his children, and you are one."

Jason sat in awe at what Pops had just said to him. This was the first time that anyone had ever said anything like that to him in a while. He then knew exactly what he had to do. He would have to give up his gay life style. He did not want to be gay anymore, so he decided to give up on this life of supposed sin. Meeting Jesus at those pearly gates was now a number one priority to him, and he would make it happen.

That Sunday, Pops, Larry, and Jason all went to the church on the hill for service. Jason was very determined at this point to change his life around. They all piled into the pew in the second row from the front. People were milling around, and some would walk past Jason and recognize him from several years ago. Jason hardly knew half the people that came up to him.

When the pastor read the first scripture Jason's head was very confused, and almost impressed with the apparent mighty ability of God. Of course, with Jason's luck, the entire sermon was about the fallacies of homosexuality. Jason at first was resisting everything said, but then remembered he was supposed to be dumping that lifestyle. One particular thing the priest said stayed with Jason for the next month and a half. That phrase was "Once the demon is inside of you, even the mighty power of God cannot remove it from you."

He would constantly battle with this phrase night and day until one day he realized that homosexuality was not a demon. The Christian church made it sound like it was some kind of unholy activity taken upon and commanded by demons. Jason knew otherwise.

He also came to some self-realization that homosexuality was not something that one decides on. A person does not sit there and think,

"Gee I want to be a homo; I will be a homo from now on, so I can be discriminated against and live a hard, almost loveless, life."

No, of course it doesn't work that way. All along Jason had thought he could change it, and now finally he realized that he couldn't. This then marked a turning point in his life with this newfound truth.

Chapter 9

With Jason's new realization, life began to take some drastic turns. The first thing that he did was step on the scale. Seeing that he had gained forty pounds since he last weighed himself he wanted to step into action. He began drinking only milk and water. Taking walks to the Indian tower only about a quarter of a mile from his house proved valuable as well. The Indian tower was a two-story tower situated on the top of a big hill that allowed you to look out into two neighboring cities. The simple fact of realizing the truth of homosexuality is what gave Jason that extra push that he needed to start taking action. He worked on his mannerisms and physical presentation, starting with shopping for some real clothes.

The days were getting warmer and longer as the school year came to a close. Jason always loved this time of the year because he didn't have to put up with Seth. Jason hated the kid, but didn't have the guts to stand up to him. Seth was constantly getting more and more built with every day that passed. No matter; Jason knew that it did not really matter your physical strength, rather your inner strength is what counted.

With the close of the school year Jason began to prepare for his birthday party. He decided that he was going to have a fruity party to see if anyone would notice. Jason was finally coming around to fully accepting the fact that he was gay. He had accepted it in the past, but not fully. He was ashamed of what he was, he told no one, and acted offended if anybody asked. Now, however, he was learning more ways to cope with other's opinions and he was becoming more comfortable with his own sexuality.

At the store, Jason picked up a bunch of stuff to get for the party. He got fresh pineapple, watermelon, cantaloupe, strawberries, blueberries and raspberries, along with a big tub of ice cream. Jason spent the rest of the day making pre-party preparations, such as tables, chairs, and stringing festive lights. He brought down his boom box, speakers, and CD adapter for entertainment. When he had all of the dishes clean that would be needed, he retired to his room.

People began to show up for the party around five-thirty. Jacquelyn showed up first, and then some of her friends. Everyone showed up one after the other, all with gifts for Jason. He got a lot of money, and clothes for his birthday. Everyone enjoyed the fruit and Elica was the only one to say anything about it being "fruity." Everyone was acting really goofy, and Jason had so much fun knowing that his friends were having fun. The amount of friends that he now had compared to last year at this time was astonishing and was put into perspective when the whole backyard was filled with people. Jason spent most of the time just milling around and talking to everyone that was there.

Elica then took him to the side and walked him around to the garden that Jason had in his back yard. Here she pointed at some bushes and asked him if he saw anything. He said he did, and stood looking interested for a few moments before he headed back to the party with Elica. He assumed that she was pointing at some "fairies" that were dancing around the tops of the bushes, so he let her know that he saw some "fairies" and she began to beam.

By the time they got back to the party there was a dance competition started. Cleo was trying to show these three other girls how to really move like a snake. Now the other three girls were taking turns with different dance moves to the music that was playing. Everyone else was just lounging around having a good time with smiles on everyone's face. When someone came up to him and let him know that she was leaving, Jason ran to get the cake and ice cream. Everyone became eager to get this food, as it was to die for. The cake was homemade by Jason, and then he topped it with a scoop of ice cream with a strawberry on top, and either blueberries or raspberries on the sides.

People hurried over to get some of the cake because the ice cream was beginning to melt. To finish off the party Jason had planned a fireworks display, and it turned out great. Everyone wanted to get pictures, so they all posed in several different ways for several different cameras. It was a lot of fun for Jason hearing the constant chatter, and the music in the background made the mood right for a perfect party. The Christmas lights cast a majority of the dim soft light upon the party scene, but the laughter that rose above the talking was by far the most rewarding of all the aspects. The fact that there was absolutely no food left after the party was also a good sign that the party was a success. Cleo was the last person to leave, besides Elica. When Cleo finally left the party, Elica and Jason began to clean up the mess. When they were finally finished cleaning and taking down the lights they decided to go down to the diner.

On the way down to the diner, Jason saw Mary, Tameera's mother, who quickly pulled over only a few feet in front of the two. She got out of the car, her face red as ever, and she started screaming, crying and running towards him. He quickly discovered why she was acting the way she was.

"Oh! God! Jason, Grammy is in the hospital because Tameera beat the living daylights out of her. Oh God, Jason, she ran away and I called the ambulance, and police…" she said, pausing only to blow her nose, and then looked up at Jason with a completely different demeanor about her. "She's with that nigger!"

Jason was taken aback at the last thing that came out of her mouth. He could not believe that she would use that word; it definitely was not like Mary to say that. He knew that Mary was talking about

Tameera's most recent boyfriend named Vinny. Vinny was a big oaf that didn't really do anything. He was a big black boy whose body was disproportionate, and whose face slanted severely to a point at his nose. He was definitely the worst boyfriend Tameera had ever had. He had no intelligence about him and when he talked he mumbled and managed somehow to have saliva running from the corner of his mouth all the time.

"Oh my God, why did she do that?"

"I found out that the little slut is pregnant! Jason, she put my mother in the hospital!" Mary screamed, putting her arms around him and sobbing into his shoulder.

"Well, I am going to come over tomorrow and we can talk and try to call her then, okay?" Jason said, trying to comfort and calm her down.

"Okay, well um, Mike is coming over tomorrow also, so I'll ask him to pick you up," Mary said, stepping back into the car. She then uttered a crackly groan and said, "Thank you." She hurriedly got back into her car and pulled away from them just as fast as she had stopped.

"Don't even ask," Jason said to Elica, because she had an unmistakably confused look on her face. She just shrugged and the two continued their walk to the diner. Upon reaching the diner they discovered a post-party. Everybody that was at Jason's party regrouped at the diner later that evening. After the quick stop at the diner, everyone piled into cars to go over to the pool hall.

It had been a very long time since he played pool, but with just a few pointers from Elica and one other guy, Jason was on his way. Jason really did not mind this game, as he had always seen it as pointless as basketball. Now, however, he realized the skill and intellect that was needed in order to get the ball where you wanted it to go. Jason was unable to focus on the game he was playing as he kept thinking about Tameera and why she would run away. From being over there every day, Jason was really surprised because Tameera didn't seem like the kind to do something like that. In fact, she appeared to deeply love her mother and Grammy, and to run away on the day of her best friend's birthday party?! How could she? Something was not right, and why did she get pregnant for a second time?

Before he knew it, Jason had lost his fifth game against Elica and their hour was up. They all paid the guy upfront but hung around a little longer to talk to everyone else that was there. Elica was chatting up a storm with her friends, who were all dressed in dark black clothing with piercings on every square inch of their bodies. Jason settled into a short bar stool that was placed next to the center bar that wrapped around the casher. Jason then began to look around and take in his surroundings. He noticed the nine pool tables, and the one that was different was situated in the back of the hall. This table was in front of a large mirror that made the place look two times its actual size. The bar and pillars that went up from the bar were made of a nice light wood that you could see was slightly darker up near the top from cigarette smoke. The whole place was under a dingy atmosphere of cigarette smoke, and the sound of the juke box was barely audible over the sound of all the balls hitting together.

While his eyes were wandering around the hall, he was left in social silence when he began thinking about the recent unfortunate happenings of his life. His sister gets hit by car, then rumors begin, and then more rumors start. He overreacted to Adrian, which sent him running, and now Tameera runs away. Just as he was beginning to slip into a thick depression, Elica came over and got him. She knew something was wrong and was not about to let him go without talking.

"What's up?" she asked.

"Nothing," Jason said, looking down and silently putting on his coat.

"Jason, you can't lie to me. I know you better than that," she said, pointing a finger at Jason.

"I dunno, it's just I've been thinking about a lot of things lately," he said, going over these things in his head again.

"Like what?"

"Well, it was set off by me finding out Tameera ran away."

"Hey, don't let that get you down, it is your birthday and so…"

"—Party," Jason butted in, to make it clear his birthday was a full month before.

"Sorry, birthday *party*, and so you should be happy…Look, I know she is a really good friend to you and all, but worry about it tomorrow, please? For me?"

"Okay," Jason said, looking up at Elica, "…but it is gonna be hard."

When Jason got home, he went directly up to his room. Upon opening the door, Snickers gave a long drawn out meow while looking up at her daddy. He came in and locked the door behind him without a word. He didn't even smoke a cigarette, instead he went right to sleep with only a single tear escaping his eye.

Chapter 10

A violent knocking on the door woke Jason up with a start. When he realized what was going on, he got out of bed and went to the door.

"Jason!" Melissa's voice came from the other side, "Mary's on the phone for you!" she said as loud as she could so that he would hear her. He was surprised at hearing her voice, as this was the first time that she was able to come up the attic steps since getting hit by a car. Jason flung open the door and bound past Melissa to get down the stairs.

"Jason?" Mary asked in a crackled voice.

"Yeah!" Jason stated, waiting for an explanation as to what was going on. Jason really cared and wanted to do anything possible for Tameera. He had over time become extremely good friends with her, and they saw each other nearly every day.

Tameera was very close to Jason and loved to tell him her secrets, and he loved to tell her his. This trust was never broken. Jason was there through her three boyfriends—Colin, Tyler, and Vinny. In fact, they were such good friends that when Tyler came over during exams, he let them have sex on his couch in his room. Tameera even let Jason sit there and watch this encounter. He did not want to watch, so he turned on the television. The whole entire time Jason was wishing he was her, and then began to plan on jumping Tyler. Surprisingly, Jason did not feel uncomfortable sitting there while this was going on right behind him.

The trust between Jason and Tameera was great and continued to grow. He would often go to her house and drink with her and her boyfriend at the time. He didn't smoke with her very often, but when he did it was all about laughter. Jason's life had really altered with having the friends he did. He gave up on church completely, began drinking alcohol and wound up smoking pot. He didn't smoke very often, but the point was that he did. Tameera was always there for Jason and he really needed it. He was there for her when she needed him, as she often had. This friendship was the best ever, as it involved a little give and a little take. That's why Jason couldn't figure out why Tameera hadn't called him yet telling him where she was.

The years seemed to fly with Tameera at his side. They would play, laugh, and joke. It did turn into serious conditions sometimes though. He had seen her hit her mother and grammy before. He thought it was bad, but never really got involved. The long summer days were made bearable with Tameera. One summer's day, when Jason was at Tameera's house all day, she saw that he was interested in the piano. He sat down and played "Ode to Joy" by Beethoven. When he was done, Tameera sat down and played "Moonlight Sonata" by Beethoven and "The Turkish March" by Mozart.

"I didn't know you played the piano," Jason said, looking amazed at Tameera.

"Yeah, I took lessons since I was twelve," she said, looking at him with a smile stretching across her face.

"Wow, can you teach me how to play that first one?" Jason asked with a sudden spark of interest.

"Sure, I'll teach you for half an hour, and then you can give me a back massage," Tameera said, looking at his fingers.

"Deal!" Jason said, excited. It had been a very long time since he had actually learned how to play a song on the piano. His grandmother was his past teacher. She taught him everything he knew. Now as the sound of the piano filled the house it was so relaxing and calm. The sound of the piano, the feeling of the ivory keys, and the feeling of the wooden bench beneath him all brought back good old memories. Now he was making new memories in front of the piano with Tameera.

That half hour wasn't very long, but the next one was (as it lasted for an hour and a half!) as he sat there cracking Tameera's back and massaging it thoroughly with cocoa-butter. He gave her a facial, leg, foot, and scalp massage. Almost a full body massage is what she got for teaching him for that short time. When he was done, she was telling him about how much she appreciated him and how good it was to have him as a friend. He then lay next to her on his back, and picked up a stuffed monkey she had and placed it on his chest. He didn't even think twice about being in the same bed as her. He was comfortable with it, and she was too. He then looked over at her and gazed into her brown eyes.

"I think I realize why I'm so happy when I'm around you and why I'm so protective of you…" Jason said looking directly into her eyes and never daring to look away. "I think I love you. Not like girlfriend–boyfriend, but like family," he quickly added, to make sure she didn't get freaked out.

Just then she pushed her eyebrows together and up and said, "Awwww, Jason, that's the sweetest thing anyone ever said to me and it makes it better, because I think you really do." With that she stood up and went over to the door and closed it. She turned around and looked at Jason. "What I'm about to tell you cannot be repeated to anyone, do you hear me?" she said, stepping closer with every word.

"I promise," Jason swore.

"Well I wasn't sure before but now I'm pretty sure… Umm… Jason…" she said, holding both of his hands.

"What?" Jason said, thinking that saying he loved her may have been a very wrong move.

"Jason, I'm pregnant, and I want to know if you want to be the godfather," she said with a hopeful smirk running across her face.

Jason had no real clue on how he should react to this news, because he was upset that she was pregnant at the young age of sixteen, but excited for her at the same time. So he hugged her close.

"Aww, oh my God! Tameera! I love you! Of course I want to be his godfather, oh my God! This is so amazing, congratulations!" Jason was shrieking, on the verge of tears with pure joy and of heartache of having to watch her go through this. After the initial shock, Jason began to ask questions. "Who's the father?"

"Vinny is," she said, very happy to answer his questions.

"How far along are you?"

"Two months, we went to Planned Parenthood and got tested."

"Boy or girl?"

"Dunno yet, it's too early to tell."

"Any names picked out?"

"Nope."

Just then it hit him—what was her mother going to think? She thought her daughter was still a virgin; what was Grammy going to think. "Who all knows?"

"You, Vinny, and Grammy"

"Isn't Grammy gonna tell your mom?"

"No. She promised she wouldn't, but she said she won't lie to her own daughter if she starts to ask questions when my stomach gets big and bulky."

"True, true." The sad reality was starting to settle in. This girl's life was going to take a very abrupt turn and it was not going to be easy. "Well, I will stick by you all the way through to the end, even if Vinny, whom I dislike, doesn't."

Tameera just laughed, and Jason let a smirk appear on his face, but his mind was in a whirl. He couldn't believe that his best friend in the whole entire world just got knocked up by some jerk off who couldn't even think. Why would she do something like that. She was so beautiful. He looked at her and did not see any sign of preparation. A single tear appeared in his eye as he began to prepare to suffer with Tameera.

That next day Jason began training at a nearby gas station. This new employment venture took away from his social time with

Tameera. Jason actually really enjoyed his job there. The people that he worked with were awesome and the customers were all fairly nice. Ever since Tameera told him about his godchild, he always had a smile on his face. He realized that Vinny would hardly be a father, so Jason became very excited just thinking about this. He had always wanted to be a father, and he figured this would be about as close as he could get to the real experience. Jason was so excited that he began doing extensive research on early childhood care. He got a bunch of his mom's baby supplies together from when he was a baby to prepare for this newborn ray of sunshine.

Jason went to work after spending hours in the attic looking for baby clothes. He was successful in finding an old walker that he could definitely use at one point or another. It was the first night that he would be working by himself, so he really hoped that Tameera would stop by. Time flew by as he seemed to be so busy, and the night was filled with one problem after another. Later that night he looked out as a pair of headlights caught his attention. The door opened and in came Tameera. She came into the doors with a little less hyper energy than usually accompanied her.

"Hey, what's up? I'm sorry I haven't been able to call you at...hey, what's wrong?" Jason asked, now looking at her with concern.

"Jason, you might want to sit down..." Tameera said, putting her hand out to hold his.

"I can't, just tell me what's wrong." Then it happened, almost all too fast. Something that he had been standing strong against his entire life, his best friend just did to his godchild.

"Jason, I got an abortion today." Jason's face quickly turned red, and the tears rushed to his eyes.

"You did what?!" Jason asked, trying to hold back the tears. "Oh my god, how could you? Do you realize that you asking me to be the godfather was the best thing that has happened to me...ever!" He cried as he put his head in his arms, and he felt his throat go into his stomach and his heart get ripped in half. He almost completely collapsed as he could hardly breathe. The tears poured and poured out of him. "And now you take that away from me!" Jason said, now feeling his sadness quickly turning into rage. "Somebody like me who will never have children of my own because I can't, and you are going to do something so stupid as to kill and take for granted something that I can never have!?" He was angry because his best friend had just murdered the only truly good thing that Jason was looking forward to in his life.

"Vinny thought it would be a good idea," she said, rubbing Jason's back. She was crying a little too, realizing now what she had done.

"You're gonna listen to that retard?" he said, now fuming with anger at her stupidity. "Tameera! He can't even say his own name!" Tameera smirked, but it wasn't meant for a laugh. Jason's heart was truly broken, but he had to quickly straighten up, watching a customer walking towards the door. "I think it would be best if you left now," Jason said, no longer looking at her.

"Jason, come on, don't be mean to me."

"Tameera…you murdered the only good thing to happen to me."

"What do you mean, 'murder'? I should never have told you!" Tameera said, now getting angry.

"Tell me or not, your conscience would still eat away at you."

With that Tameera stood there and glared at him before she left in a storm. Jason could not believe what had just happened and absolutely hated Tameera for it. Jason did not talk to her again until the day before his birthday party. He then apologized for overreacting and they hugged and made up. She was still going out with Vinny and had gained a little weight.

"Well, Mike told me that she was pregnant, and he said that she had an abortion once before!" Mary began crying. "Jason, did you know this?"

"Yes, that abortion was my godchild," Jason confessed to her.

"What? She said you were going to be its godfather and then she killed it! Jason, that was my grandson!"

"Yeah, it was really sad, but why did she run away?"

"I'll tell you when you get here, Mike is on his way for you."

"Oh okay, well I guess I'll see you soon then," Jason said, then hung up the phone. He stared off into space trying to figure out why she would have run away.

Two hours passed before Mike actually got there to pick him up. Mike was a gay boy from a nearby town who was attractive. He had ocean blue eyes and brown hair that he would get frosted and spike. The thick stubble made for a deep shadow effect, essentially framing his face. His jaw jutted out and his bottom lip curled down slightly. He was big boned, but in good shape. He did have a lot of hair, with a thick matting of hair covering his arms at the age of eighteen. He was always tan, no matter what season. Jason was, however, turned off by his drug abuse. He was always high on crack, coke or pot. He even ate mushrooms and took ecstasy pills. When he wasn't wasted, he was trying to kill himself. After Jason's explosion over the abortion, Tameera became best friends with him, leading her into a major drug problem.

The two did not stay very long at Tameera's house because Mike didn't want to stay very long. Mary told Jason about what had happened two days before. Tameera told Mary about her being pregnant and Mary went crazy, calling her a slut and easy. Tameera then went crazy and hit her mother, and Grammy got involved to try and stop it. When Tameera punched her, she was knocked out cold. Mary ran for the phone, only to be jumped on by Tameera. She then ripped a large chunk of her hair out before leaving with Vinny.

"Oh Jason, could you please try and call her? Here is her father's cell phone number; the cops said she's there," Mary pleaded with Jason. He took the number and put it in his pocket, hoping to call it soon. He then figured out why she gained weight. She was pregnant again and couldn't hide it from her mother. Grammy told Mary because she was worried about Tameera.

Mike decided to take the highway back to town; at least that's what Jason thought. He passed the exit that he should have taken, but Jason didn't say anything to him. He had figured Mike was going to take a back road. They wound up in the big city with buildings rising high and traffic scrunched together into a tight street. He had no idea what was going on and even spoke up while they were still on they highway. They pulled up in front of a house in the row house section. "Okay, um Jason, just wait right here, and um, listen to some music or something." Jason watched Mike go up the steps and knock on the door. It was kind of funny to watch Mike standing there in all of his paranoia.

After two long minutes the door swung open and Mike stepped inside as a black man closed the door behind him. Only a few seconds passed before Jason began to get nervous. He could hear the bass system of a car coming right towards him. Jason just knew they would be going to the same place. Jason couldn't believe he didn't see it earlier. Mike was doing a drug deal or was this a gay hangout. Jason leaned a little more towards the first idea. That is when Jason really began to get worried and scared. Just then, two kids got out of the loud car and went to walk up the steps. Jason, as quickly as he could, put his seat back to try and prevent detection. He looked up in time to see the two backs of heads go into the house. But no! Jason would never believe it! Had he just seen whom he thought he saw? Jason became really pale just thinking of this person and Mike. Knowing that this kid and Mike were about to encounter each other gave Jason the chills. Never! This person was mean spirited, so why would he be coming here, and what was going on? Jason could not stop thinking about him, when he saw activity at the door again.

Mike stepped out and turned around, talking to somebody. That somebody then came to the door and gave Mike a kiss. Jason was sitting up now in disbelief. This could not be possible; he couldn't look away just then; his stomach did a somersault. This guy just saw Jason and shut the door in a hurry. Mike looked down at his truck in surprise at seeing Jason's head sitting there in plain view. Mike came running to the truck, got in and quickly pulled away. "God, I'm so stupid!" Mike said.

"Why…and what the hell was that stop about?" Jason asked.

"I should have either told you to come in with me or put your seat back so no one would see you."

"Why?"

"Dunno, they're weird like that, but I got some weed! You wanna smoke?"

"I thought you didn't have any money?" Jason asked, confused.

"Nope, I got it with my looks," Mike said, spreading a smile across his face and muttering an "Owa mya gawda."

"I don't think I want to know," Jason responded. He noticed erratic wet marks on Mike's shirt. That was enough to explain everything.

"So, do you know that kid that answered the door? He likes everyone, but he didn't seem happy to see you. What are you, an ex or something?" Mike asked, looking over at Jason while packing a bowl.

"No, no, never saw him before," Jason lied.

Chapter 11

Sunday night came around and Jason was still trying to understand why he had seen that guy at that particular house. Not to mention why he had kissed another guy. Jason just wanted to get away from all of this thinking, so he called Elica to see what she was doing. She wanted him to come over promptly, so he did. As soon as he walked into her house, he received a very large hug. Elica was another great friend that Jason had and really enjoyed spending time with. She was an attractive young girl with black hair and a really nice body. Her eyes were dark brown, and she had light freckles all over her face and arms.

"Do you have any money on you?" Elica asked.

"Umm, yeah. I have about five dollars," Jason responded.

"Okay, good, hold on, let me get dressed," she said, scrambling towards her bedroom. "Oh yeah, do you want to go to the diner?"

"Sure," he said, knowing that this was just about the only thing to do in this little town. He felt bad for her because she always wanted to get out of the house, but could not do so with little to do. It didn't take long before the two were on their way to the diner for their gossip session. Jason was gay, so he really didn't mind the drama all that much, but it did get a little annoying to him after a short while.

Jason felt that he could really talk to Elica about serious happenings and topics and she would understand. That is why Jason really did like to talk with her and share with her some of his experiences. Jason walked with Elica down to the diner and walked back with her later. On the way home the two began talking about religion. Jason explained to her the way he felt about God, Jesus and the Holy Spirit. She then explained to him everything she believed.

While Elica was talking about her religion, Jason fell head first into her way of thinking. It all made sense. Some things that she had said he didn't agree with one hundred percent, but he could change that if he converted into her religion. "I think you are kind of Wiccan," Elica said to Jason as they reached her house.

"What makes you say that?" Jason asked, perplexed.

"Well, some of the stuff that you believe in and have experienced...I mean geez, you have all of these magical herbs growing in your garden, and you can see fairies. Is that fate or what!" she finished, with a smile crossing her face.

"Okay, yes, I will admit that it would be interesting to be Wiccan, and to be able to perform magic, however, I do not want to sell my soul to the devil."

"What! You can tell you were an uber Christian."

"What do you mean?"

"Well, we don't sell our souls to Satan. In fact, there is no such thing as a Satan. There is an evil, and there is a good, but each is not pure in that form. It's called the ying-yang effect."

"What exactly do you mean by that?" Jason asked, raising his eyebrows.

"There is a little bad in everything good, and there is a little good in everything bad," she said, throwing her purse onto her kitchen table, after scrounging through it for her cigarettes. Jason lit up a cigarette with her. "We believe in the god and goddess, you envision them however you want to see them as."

This struck Jason as a bit odd, as he was not used to a unstructured religion.

"Unlike the Christian god, who is a man and domineering, along

89

with all good, oh no child, that's just not the way things work around here."

Jason had no idea how to react to this information, so he laughed, which wasn't taken very nicely by Elica.

Jason and Elica continued to talk about misconceptions about witchcraft and other religions well into the morning. He then agreed to have his tarot cards read by her. She began by lighting a piece of charcoal that began to spark. She then threw herbs onto the charcoal and they were soon smoldering. She had lain out a black cloth and then lit the different colored candles. She then lay out the cards after he personally selected ten cards. He was told that he had a horrific past, a bad present, and would have a bad future, but only for a small time. Jason was then told that he would achieve what he really wanted and live happily. The next card that Elica turned over was the death card; Jason's heart leapt at the sight of this card. When he jokingly said he was going to die, Elica corrected him.

"Just because it's the death card does not mean that you are going to die. It actually means that something will come to an end, something would have been overcome, the death of the old and in with the new. It means several different things. In fact, it rarely acts as a card illustrating your death," she stated, pushing a loose hair strand back behind her ear. "Now, the god and goddess want you to know that…" She began as she turned over the last card, "…they want you to know that you should begin to live your life a little more excitingly so as to accomplish this goal you are to accomplish." Elica stopped, looking up interested in Jason's reaction. He just looked up at her with a smile on his face, assuring her that he was okay.

"Now remember," Elica began, "…this is your future, and you can change it if you feel the need to." Jason was actually a little comforted by knowing this, as that death card was definitely a shock. They spent the rest of the morning talking about Wicca. Elica began teaching him how to perform magic and basic spell construction. Jason lit a cigarette and began on his journey home.

Monday night, Jason made plans with Stitla, from the gas station, to go over to her house and drink. Jason headed over immediately after work and they all began. Stitla brought down the bong and Jason took a few rips off of it, just as he was beginning to feel the effects of the alcohol. Ron, Stitla's flamer roommate, was playing on the computer, drinking his beer. Ron was a scary person. He was skinny, except for his gut, was about thirty-nine years old, and his top teeth were fake. He had a really raspy voice, and was so gay it was not even funny. He was, however, dating Stitla's other roommate, Adrianna. Approximately two hours passed by when they were all pretty drunk. Stitla was called upstairs by Adrianna. Those two began to talk very animatedly. Jason heard them talking and thought they would never stop. Ron soon stood up and went over to the kitchen and prepared himself a drink. When it was prepared, he went over and sat on the couch across from Jason.

The news was talking about Catholic priests getting into trouble for molesting young boys. "I don't see why they would get in trouble for that," Ron spoke up. "I mean, all of those boys were like fifteen, sixteen, they wanted it!" Ron said, becoming aggravated. "If a sixteen- or seventeen-year-old boy doesn't say anything when you suck on their cock, they obviously want it. Right?"

Jason just agreed with him, even though he really didn't. The two had been debating the news when nasty thoughts began to enter Jason's mind. Soon enough his body became excited, and the old man saw this.

"Are you hitting on me?" he asked.

Jason responded quickly, "No...but what if I was?"

"What if you were?" Ron repeated, then took a puff of his cigarette and looked at Jason with lustrous eyes. He then stood up with one hand down his shorts and walked over to the television. He bent over and turned it off, and then stood at the bottom of the couch continuing to stare at Jason in the same way. "I wanna see how big this monster is," he said, getting a little closer. "Come on, I've heard so much about how big it is, and now I want to see it."

Inside of Jason's head, thoughts were trying to force their way through, but because of the substances he was on, he was unable to think clearly. Before he knew it, Jason had unzipped his pants, and

Ron was descending quickly to that area. He quickly put out his cigarette he was smoking earlier and began to work.

"You're not gonna tell anyone, right?" Ron asked before continuing.

"No," Jason quickly replied.

Jason zipped up his pants and lit a cigarette as fast as he could. Ron sat back smoking a cigarette, and looking like he was in complete ecstasy said, "Mmm, a tummy full of that stuff sure can make you feel young again," he said, licking his lips and really freaking Jason out. "How many times has somebody done that to you?" Ron asked.

"Four or five times," Jason lied. That had never been done to him before; this was indeed the first time. The whole entire time all he could think about was 'So this is what it feels like'. Now that it was over he really started to freak out. One, Ron's girlfriend was Jason's friend. Two, he was thirty-nine with missing teeth. Thirdly, he wasn't even attractive. Jason stayed as they all went upstairs. Ron was then acting like he was in control of Jason and that was when he decided to leave.

The next day came and Jason went to see Stitla as quickly as possible. He confessed to her what happened the previous night. She was appalled at Ron, but then confessed to Jason that she had sex with him on several occasions. This new information comforted Jason in no way at all. The two sat there first infuriated with Ron's actions and then sad thinking about Stitla's best friend, Adrianna. She has been going out with Ron for about two years now, and was totally ignorant about what had been going on. They both wanted to tell her so bad, but decided against it because she might be severely hurt. Shelley, Stitla's friend, was there and encouraged them to go to Adrianna and tell her, but they couldn't. Shelley had, over time from going over to Stitla's house, become a really good friend to Jason. She was always there and she really had a good head on her shoulders. Instead of Jason counseling everyone else, she would counsel him. He turned to her for everything because he knew that she was a dependable person.

Jason couldn't stop talking to her about what had happened, and he was really upset. "I didn't even like it," Jason admitted. "Like, I got a release, but it was not enjoyable. In fact, when I was walking home last night I was seriously questioning if I was really gay or not," Jason admitted.

Stitla, Shelley and Jason conversed about this for close to three hours, but dared not act any differently towards Ron.

Later that night, Jason ventured on over to Elica's with plans to tell her all about it. When Jason finished, Elica reacted a little differently than others would. "Woohoo! Jason got some! Ha ha ha, alright Jason, you're growing up so fast."

"No Elica, it isn't cool. He's like, thirty-nine!"

"Yeah, can you say child molester? But hey, you got some! Woohoo!"

"Yeah I guess I did, didn't I," Jason responded, in a way that made Elica forget about it rather quickly. Jason then told her about the fertility spell he did for her in hopes she might have a successful pregnancy. Elica was only twenty-three and had been pregnant three times. All three times that she had gotten pregnant she had a miscarriage. These three repeated happenings had hurt her very much. Now all that she wanted to do was have a healthy baby that would live. Jason figured he would help her out and performed a fertility spell for her.

"Blessed be!" Elica said, while holding Jason in her arms. "Thank you so much! Do you know how much that means to me?"

"A lot, I'm sure," Jason responded. Elica was making something that smelled really good so Jason asked if he could have some.

"Sure, if you don't mind eating off of a paper plate and using plastic utensils," she said, getting out plates, forks and knives.

"I don't mind, I'm so used to them," Jason responded. "I remember when I first came out to my mom. Oh my God, did she go nuts. I had to eat off of paper plates, drink from plastic cups, and eat with plastic utensils. She was so afraid that I was going to spread AIDS to everyone in my family, and she also said that she didn't know where my dirty mouth had been lately and wanted to be safe," Jason finished, actually smiling at Elica's reaction to this.

"Eww! I wanna kill her!" Elica said, face screwed up in disgust. "Can I shoot her with a sniper rifle?" Elica asked, eyebrows raised, and a look of pure joy spreading over her face thinking of killing his mother.

"No, you may not! Even though my mom is extremely screwed up, you may not shoot her, 'cause I still love her. She is my mother and nothing can change that. Besides, she doesn't even think I'm gay anymore," Jason said laughing. "I convinced her that I was straight because I liked Shelley! I told her that I never really had an attraction to guys, it was just I wasn't attracted to girls in school! And she bought the whole thing, thank God!"

"And goddess," Elica quickly added. "Well duh! She's an uber-Christian; she doesn't know anything about anything. Geez, do I ever hate Christians," Elica finished with a quick little laugh. It wasn't much longer till Jason left Elica's and began his little trek home.

Jason walked everywhere because he didn't have a car yet, but every time he would wind up walking it was its own little adventure. On warm days Jason would take the really long route home, just for the variation. He would do so on cold days as well, just not as often. Upon walking home Jason's eyes would often wander about, taking in things he never noticed before. Hidden doors, extra houses, architectural outcroppings, graffiti, and hidden passageways between buildings were just a few of the things that he would notice. Each time he took a walk he learned more about his community. He liked this little town, and there were so many aesthetic facades, lamp posts and horse tie rings. The only thing Jason didn't like was the fact that everyone was biased, and there were little to no gay people residing in the area. This town was actually nicely populated, but it had nothing for the kids in town to do. Jason was growing out of this small town community, and began thinking about the city. He knew that there he may just be able to be who he really was, gay Jason. When he got home he lay down on the top of his covers and cuddled next to Snickers, as his thoughts continued to fall back to Ron and Adrianna.

A week passed before Jason was back to visit Ron. Jason had a weakness, and he had no outlet for his sexual desires except for Ron.

Jason rang the doorbell and walked in when Ron answered the door. Stitla had given Jason a cell phone for his birthday, so Jason went there to pick up the accessories. Adrianna was off at work, and Ron was the only one around. Ron was playing video games upstairs, so Jason sat and chatted with him for a little while. Jason then went downstairs and put in porn to watch. He sat there watching and playing when he heard Ron coming down the steps. He then turned off the television and picked up a newspaper. When Ron got downstairs, he asked Jason what he was doing. Jason said, "Nothing, just reading the newspaper." But Ron did not believe him.

Jason didn't finish, but soon joined Ron upstairs where he continued to play his video game. "I shaved there," Jason began. "Now it is uncomfortable and red."

"Oh yeah..."Ron said, looking at the television screen, and then his eyes drifted over to Jason, "...lemme see it," he said while laughing. "Aww, poor thing, let me see it."

"No, I'm embarrassed. It's all red," Jason said. "Why don't you let me see yours, if you shave?"

With that Ron stood up and walked over to Jason while lowering his pants.

Time had passed when Jason stopped what he was doing, feeling guilty, and said, "What about Adrianna?"

Ron wanted Jason to continue, but said, "She's just like my old girlfriend. If she can't tell something's going on and it's right in front of her, then fuck that stupid bitch."

With that comment Jason looked up at him with his eyebrows raised and said that he had to leave. Just then the front door to the apartment slammed open and footsteps were heard running up the steps. Jason struggled to get himself together, but couldn't before Adrianna walked in the door.

Chapter 12

The initial explosion was expected, as Adriana walked in on both guys with everything exposed and on the same bed. Jason had tried to hurriedly cover up, but couldn't thanks to his clumsy nervousness. Very quickly objects began flying across the room at the two of them. Jason could understand completely, but ran out of the house as quickly as possible. He ran to the gas station where Stitla was working. He filled her in on all of the facts. Jason couldn't even finish before she was calling people to see if someone could come in and work for her. Adrianna was soon at the gas station and was inside before Jason had a chance to hide.

"Stitla! Did you know that Ron and Jason are fucking?" Adriana asked with hands flailing and a very heavy breathing pattern.

"He told me once before, yes," Stitla said honestly.

"Oh my God!" Adriana screamed. "Why didn't you tell me? If anyone, I figured you would be honest with me!"

"I didn't want to be the one to hurt you," Stitla continued.

"Well I'm hurt more now! Did he ever do anything with you?" Adriana asked, holding her hands up in the air. Stitla didn't respond. "DID HE EVER DO ANYTHING WITH YOU?" Adriana screamed at the top of her lungs. Stitla began to shake and she pushed her hair back with her hands before she actually responded.

"There was penetration once," Stitla said as the tears began to fill her eyes.

"Oh my God, oh my God! Well I'll be back, he left, and I am going to find him!" Adriana said, "This is just too fuckin' much!" she screamed before slamming the door open and running out to her car. Stitla continued to shake and cry behind the counter when her replacement showed up. Jason was going to walk Stitla home, but didn't after she told him to go home and call her later.

Jason continued to talk to Stitla, but hadn't talked to Ron or Adrianna for a long time. Stitla would fill Jason in on the happenings of what was going on, but Jason could not communicate with them. Ron had convinced Adriana that Jason was a psychopath. She was convinced that he was so crazy that if he believed something happened it really happened in his eye. He also convinced her that Jason was a habitual liar, and over exaggerated. Since Jason couldn't hang out at Stitla's as much, his friendship with Elica increased. He was almost always over at her house, talking with her and her husband, which would easily increase anyone's friendship with someone.

Elica absolutely loved Jason; she called him her little flamer, he called her his fag hag. They were always down at the diner, which gave Jason plenty of time to make fun of people in the way Elica delighted in. In order to make her laugh, all Jason would have to do is act really feminine. He mainly hung out with Elica at night and Shelley during the day. Shelley liked to live a life of luxury, which Jason liked to do as well.

Before long, Jason's last year at highschool came and went. He went into the school year with a much better perspective than he has ever had. He was going to take a heavy hit this year, taking classes like advanced physics and calculus.

By the beginning of the second semester of Jason's final year in school, he was back on talking terms with Ron and Adriana. Jason did make it known, however, that he didn't like Ron very much. He was happy to be friends with Adriana again, but hated her lying, cheating, child-molesting boyfriend. Jason could get along with him, but would injure him if the opportunity arose. Most of the rage that he felt towards Ron was because he was a child molester. Jason, having been molested when he was young, did not look too nicely upon child molesters.

The negative feelings towards Ron slowly began to dwindle. The school year had finished in what seemed like a blink of an eye, and his eighteenth birthday was coming up rapidly. He knew of two nightclubs that he would want to go to following his birthday. When he thought of going to the club he got butterflies in his stomach. He wasn't really used to being around a lot of people, loud music, and dancing.

In front of a mirror was where you would find Jason if you heard music playing in his room. He knew his birthday was approaching rapidly, and, therefore, so was the nightlife. Jason knew enough to try and prepare himself for that experience. Music videos and certain T.V. shows were his dance teachers. He watched Missy Elliot work it, Shakira shake it, and Madonna vogue. He would play the video back and forth going over the moves until he felt he did a pretty good job. Shelley would come over every now and then to do some "club" dancing with him. She taught him a lot of little dance moves that he could do. Jason was starting to feel a little better about himself as time progressed.

This year Jason's birthday passed just like any other day, with just a few "Happy Birthdays" directed towards him. This didn't bother him all too much, as his mind was on the club. It was Wednesday and the underage night was the next night at the one gay club in the nearby city. Jason called Shelley as soon as he was awake because she promised him a new outfit for his birthday. He was still talking to her when she pulled up in front of his house. He ran out to her car with a smile quickly spreading across his face.

"Where we goin'?" Shelley asked in a high pitched cartoon-like voice.

"Wal-Mart or Kohl's would be fine," Jason responded, flipping the sun visor down to check his face and hair in the mirror. Shelley looked at him with her dark brown eyes and looked back at the road. She slammed on the acceleration to get his attention.

"Like my new earrings?" she asked, looking at him quickly.

"Yeah, they're cute," Jason said, smiling at Shelley. He looked at her hair then as her earrings were little dragons. She had her black hair up tight with two chopsticks stuck in to hold it in place. She had her work uniform on, which consisted of black pants and a white dress shirt with a nice shiny black vest. Shelley worked in the local Italian restaurant. She was a very beautiful girl, with a nearly perfect figure.

They approached Kohl's after Shelley lectured Jason on how if he wants to look nice and feel good about himself he should shop at better stores than Wal-Mart, stores that were trend setters or that were quick to follow a trend. "I've never been to Kohl's," Jason admitted

"Well you're going today," Shelley said with a grin spreading across her face. The word uncomfortable would describe how Jason felt going shopping on someone else's money. Shelley had not given him a price at which she could afford, so he was shopping the clearance rack. Here he found a really nice corduroy jacket, a pair of off-white pants, and a nice black shirt to go under this outfit. The total came to only twenty dollars, which Shelley seemed happy about as well.

They pulled up in front of Jason's house, making plans for the following night. Jason was going to follow her to the club, and he would have some of his friends along in his car. Just thinking about it made his stomach do somersaults, but he was really excited and couldn't wait to go. The next day came and seemed to take forever.

Jason was dancing first thing when he woke up, and got out all of his clothes and tried to make up his mind as to exactly what outfit he was going to wear. He looked in several different fashion-conscious magazines to try and figure out what would be a good combination of clothes for this. Looking at these magazines really made him feel bad and really scruffy. These guys were all so perfect in their bodies and clothing. After ogling at these men in all their splendor he finally picked out an outfit of tight blue jeans, a red Aeropostale shirt and his white corduroy coat he bought.

Time had finally come for them all to make their way to the club. Jason was so nervous, but everyone got him pumped up so that he was excited. When they got there he heard the music halfway down the block. His stomach was really moving around now he was just so nervous. He tried to not think about this and talk to his friends, but the feeling was so overwhelming. They made it to the doors, and were asked to see their I.D.'s. After the I.D. check, they proceeded to the back of the club. Jason felt eyes with every step that he took. He noticed the black interior of the club with the carpeting on the walls. The stage was illuminated with lights of all kinds to attract the eyes and arouse the senses. There were little tables along the wall with bar stools all around. The DJ had a hutch that allowed him to look out over the entire club, and the music came powerfully from the speakers.

The club filled quickly, and they all stood at the edge of the stage as if waiting for something. Jason watched as these three guys stepped out onto the floor and began walking back and forth in a fierce manner. They were definitely fashion savvy, and were all dancing very well. Jason recognized the motions they were going through and he knew that they were vogueing. He watched in amazement, and jumped at a loud voice coming through the speakers. "ALL RIGHT EVERYBODY, ARE YOU READY FOR PUMP NIGHT?" The voice said in an announcer tone of voice. "WE HAVE A GREAT SHOW FOR YOU TO NIGHT, SO LET'S GIVE IT UP FOR MISS QUEEN OF PRIDE, VIVICA VON PETERS!"

The crowd roared, and Jason noticed the vogueing guys were clapping happily, obviously in favor of this lady.

The surprise that confronted Jason was hilarious. He had never seen a drag queen before, and then suddenly right there in front of him there was a drag queen performing to some techno song that went "...I got my pride, and no one's gonna take it away..." Jason stood, intrigued with the combination of props and the lighting. It made for such an awesome show that lasted about half an hour.

The voice came back over the speakers, "DO WE HAVE A JASON IN THE CROWD? IT'S YOUR BIRTHDAY TODAY RIGHT?" At that all of his friends pushed him out onto the stage. He was so embarrassed and the big light shone right on him, which limited his vision to about two feet in front of him. Just then a little plump drag queen with a blonde wig grabbed his hand and took the microphone.

"So, Jason I have a big question for you tonight," she said into the microphone, and looking out into the crowd, continued, "…so, do you like the penga or the fish?" Jason just stood there, and before he had a chance to say anything the DJ played a clip that said, "I'm gay." Jason pointed at the DJ and nodded his head with a big smile. The crowd began clapping, and then the drag queen took the microphone back. "Okay, so on three we are going to give you a FUCK YOU HAPPY BIRTHDAY…ONE… TWO… THREE." The whole club rang out with people screaming out. Jason turned red with embarrassment and went back to his friends all screaming.

Later in the night, after dancing with Shelley, Jason was approached by one of the three guys out on the floor vogueing before the show. "Hi, it's Jason right?"

"Yeah, it is."

"My name is Jayden."

"Hi, umm, good job out there before the show. That was really cool the way you guys were all vogueing," he said, putting a smile on his face.

"Oh that was nothing, it is really easy to do, but uh, yeah, what are you doing after the club?"

"Umm, well, I had planned on going home, but I don't really have anything planned for tomorrow. Why?"

"Well, me and my friends want to know if you would want to come over to our place."

"Okay, um sure," Jason said, not really knowing if he should be agreeing to this.

"Okay, we will find you when the club lets out then," Jayden said before walking away to go into whispers with his friends, who watched the whole thing. Jayden was a semi-attractive black boy, who had awesome green eyes that stood out even in the dark club environment. Jason went about his business and danced for what seemed like only fifteen minutes before the music stopped and everyone filed outside. When he got outside he realized how loud the music actually was. He could hear everything, but it all sounded really quiet, like someone put something over his ears.

"Shelley, I am going to follow these guys back to their place and hang out for a little bit, okay?" Jason asked her, just so that she knew where he was going.

"What about your other friends?" Shelley asked, leaning close and getting a very serious look about her.

"Oh, they are going to stay over at a friend's house here," Jason responded quickly. "The only one that is coming with me is Elica."

"Oh okay, well call me tomorrow then, okay?" she asked, just to make sure that he was going to be okay.

"All right, I will… love you," he said as he gave her a kiss on the cheek. The drive that followed was most unexpected. They wound up driving for an hour to these people's house that they did not even know. This decision that Jason made would be both the best and the worst decision he had ever made.

Through months of attending Jayden's house, Jason became what he thought was best friends with them all. Jayden wanted to get into Jason's pants, so did David, and Malik hated Jason's guts. Jayden and Malik both did drag, and were great dancers. Malik was so much better than Jayden in almost every aspect, but no one really cared. David did nothing except for sit there and gain weight. Jason wound up doing things with Jayden, and he had more fun than he thought that he would have, but then he began to change. Practically living in this house, he caught onto the strong attitude and rudeness that was constantly in the air. He never was quick witted, but eventually he got pretty good with his comebacks.

Living in this house, Jason was exposed to the side of the gay life that he did not like. Jayden and Malik both had sugar daddies, where if they wanted things or money they could get it with just a small sacrifice. Everyone that Jason ran into had sex with one of the three, and they all had sex with each other at one point or another. This never really set with Jason, but he just left it alone and tried not to talk about it. After about a month of all of this he was able to see what was going on and how much he had changed. Jason turned into what seemed like a numb person, devoid of emotion, and up for anything that he once stood up against. He was so happy to get out of that place as the stress was building up so much. He was not the same and always seemed really grumpy. When he moved out he was able to remember what it was like to be like himself again. He laughed a lot more, and had a smile on his face more often once again. The attitude never left him though, and sometimes he could get really nasty and hurt peoples feelings.

Some people loved this change in character and laughed all the time at the things he would say to other people. Jason realized that living in that house was slowly rotting away his heart, and he had to get out of there. They all thought that cheating was an okay thing, and never held any true emotions for other guys. It really did seem like they were in it for just the sex. Jason continued going to the clubs and enjoyed it a lot. He was always searching for the next boyfriend, who seemed like he would never come.

Chapter 13

Jason was driving his neighbor and friend Abby to the city to meet up with some of her friends. She had given him gas money, so he had no issue driving her. Abby had been his neighbor for years, so he was very used to her inattentiveness to reality. She kept calling the people she was supposed to be meeting, and when they did not answer for the fifth time, Jason began to wonder if they were going to stand her up.

"Do you still wanna go?" Jason asked her.

"Yeah… they'll be there," she said, looking at her phone, then exhaling long and hard.

The two had gotten to the gas station in the city and were waiting for almost forty-five minutes. Jason was convinced that no one was going to show up. "Hun, we have been here for forty five-minutes, and they have not answered your calls." Jason paused to take a sip of his blackberry lemonade. He made a face, as he was still surprised at how sweet this drink was, even though he had only two sips left.

"I am pissed!" yelled Abby, slamming her foot down on the floorboard. Just then Jason's cell phone rang, which rarely ever happened, so he dug to the bottom of his pocket to answer. He answered the phone and was surprised to hear his friend from the club on the other end.

"Que hace?" she asked in Spanish.

"Nothin! What are you doin, gurl?" Jason asked in an excited gay tone.

"Me and Josh were hangin' out, so we wanted to see what you were doing," she said, now speaking perfect English.

"Nothing really, me and my friend Abby were supposed to meet someone, but they didn't show," Jason said looking over at Abby's disappointed face.

"Wait, are you by Tenth Street?" she asked.

"Yeah, we're on Seventh."

"You should come over and hang out."

"Hold on," Jason said into the phone, before he put it down. Then to Abby he said, "Do you wanna come with me and hang out with some of my friends?"

"Are they fun?" she asked.

"Hell yeah," Jason said. "Alright, we'll be there," Jason said and hung up the phone. He started the car and they headed over to Tenth Street.

They walked into the downstairs apartment, led by the music, and were greeted with a warm welcome. Alexus, whom Jason had talked to on the phone, came running over, squealing with pleasure at seeing Jason, to give him a hug. Josh came over with arms wide and head cocked to the side.

"Hey gurl," he said to Jason.

"Hey!" Jason said, giving both a hug. "This is my friend, Abby"

"Hi," both said in unison.

"Do you want a drink?" Alexus had asked both parties.

"Sure, why not?" Abby said, raising her eyebrows. Alexus went into the refrigerator and pulled out a pitcher full of blue liquid.

"Have you ever drank absinthe?" she asked.

"No, what's absithe?" Abby asked. Jason's eyebrows had in the meantime raised, and he now looked on with wild interest at the container of blue temptation.

"Absinthe, and it's like the only alcohol that makes you hallucinate," Jason said with near passion in his voice.

"I'm down for it," Abby said, anxious to get at anything that would alter her state of mind.

"Me too, shit," Jason said, handing a paper cup to Abby and taking one for himself. As Alexus began pouring Jason noticed that other people were coming into the room.

Jason knew one as Hector, but the other one Jason had only seen around at the club. Jason's stomach lurched at the sight of him. He was Puerto Rican, and had a very well groomed goatee. His eyebrows were shaped like an eagle's wing, and he had eyelashes that were thick, well spaced, and very showy. His hazel eyes sparkled in even the faintest of light in the kitchen. He made for a beautiful piece of art, that only the god and goddess could have painted in a fit of love. Even Abby had hesitated taking a sip of her drink at the sight of this young man.

Hector was talking about how he dramatically broke up with his boyfriend when they came walking in. "...And oh my god, Danny, you should have seen his face."

Danny was not paying attention at the moment, because he caught sight of Jason. He looked at Jason's healthy figure, and loved the way his eyebrows arched, long and hard, unlike any other guy he had met. His glasses framed his wonderful brown eyes and his skin radiated health from the kitchen light. Danny looked down and laughed at what Hector had said.

Jason, having to look away to break this hypnosis, took a sip of his drink and raised his eyebrows in disbelief. While bringing down his cup, he giggled a little because Abby was now looking at Jason in disbelief of what she had just seen.

"Is he gay?" she asked Jason, but Jason wasn't sure. He had seen him quickly at the club before, but that did not necessarily mean that he was gay. When Jason had seen him at the club, he never bothered to approach him, assuming immediately that Danny would not be interested. Jason had put himself a few levels below Danny on the social food chain.

Danny just then came over and poured himself some more absinthe-spiked Kool-aid, and took a few quick glances at Jason. Jason was finding it very hard to not look at Danny, he just seemed to be a magnet to Jason's eyes. The night progressed with the five of them talking, laughing, and dancing. Danny was playing the role of DJ. Jason discovered that Danny actually lived with Josh, and there was debate between the two of them as to if they were together. Josh kept trying to steal kisses from Danny, but he kept backing off.

The light was dim, only coming from the kitchen, and it was getting into the wee hours of the morning. The absinthe was still flowing through everyone's veins. Jason hadn't had a drink for about three hours, but still continued to hear people calling his name. It had become a joke through the evening between Danny and Jason. He was convinced that it was Danny calling his name.

The futon was folded out now, and several people were laying in it. Abby, Alexus, Hector, and Danny all lay in the bed, while Jason lay on a small bed next to it. The talking had all faded away now to snoring, but Jason still lay wide-awake.

"Jason," he heard, and cursed the absinthe under his breath. It sounded like Danny, but Jason knew it wasn't. He lay thinking of Danny over and over in his mind, until he finally fell asleep.

Blue sunlight was filtering through the small basement windows when he woke up. Danny's face was immediately in front of his own, eyes still sparkling. A single cricket could be heard right outside of the apartment door, but that faded from Jason's hearing, as his heart had begun thumping fast. Danny reached over and rubbed the side of Jason's face for a second before he leaned in for a kiss. It was a quick kiss. Danny giggled and tuned over to face the other way. A very large smile came upon Jason's face, yet he lay still. Danny reached back and grabbed Jason's arm and put it around him. Jason moved closer, and strained mentally to keep his imagination from flowing. He didn't want his body to become alert, so he worked with all his might to go back to sleep.

Jason woke a few hours later to Josh coming out of the other room. "What the hell?" he asked out loud to himself. Jason kept his eyes closed but mentally prepared for a blow up. Jason's arm was still around Danny, but the covers were off, and their legs were intertwined. Josh opened the apartment door. Out of the slits in his eyelids Jason could see him turn around and look at the two on the floor. The door stayed slammed shut for a few seconds before Danny said anything.

"I better go out there," he said, raising himself off of the bed.

"Why?" Jason asked, not wanting Danny to leave his side.

"I have to…I'll be back," he said, leaning in to kiss Jason. The kiss only lasted a fraction of a second, but Jason felt like he could float. Danny lingered there for another second, as if he didn't want to stop either, before he stood up and started adjusting his clothes to make them fit perfectly. "I'll be back," he said again before he exited the door. Jason watched the door until Abby woke up two hours later. No return of Danny ever blessed that door. Jason's feelings of loss at that time was immeasurable.

The drive home seemed unbearable. Abby kept cracking jokes about the previous night. She was convinced she kept seeing a person in the closet. He seemed really sexual, and for some reason got her excited. "I mean we're talking waterfall…" Abby began laughing so hard "…but there was nobody there!" She laughed, bending over double and covering her face with her hands. She was laughing so hysterically that her eyes began to tear. "Oh squishy butt, I think I lost it."

"Squishy butt?" Jason's face screwed up at the confusion.

Then, with a Spanish/Chinese accent, she began to explain, "Yes, I nodiced dat you walk wid a squishy butt, derfor you shall be squishy butt, me friend." She continued to laugh, and placed a hand on the dashboard. Jason just went with it, he didn't find this particularly funny. His mind, however, was still with Danny.

Abby and Jason said their goodbyes when they got home, and Abby asked him if he wanted to smoke a blunt later.

"All right, maybe later then," he said before walking through the front door. Jason was walking up the attic stairs when his phone rang. It was Josh's number, and Jason knew all too well what was coming.

"Hello?" Jason answered.

"Hello, Jason?" the familiar voice asked.

"Danny?"

"Yeah, what are you doing?"

"Nothing, just chilling," Jason said, sitting excitedly on the bed.

"Do you wanna hang out later?" the crackling manly voice asked.

"Sure, but what about…?"

"Josh isn't mad, we aren't together anyway. He has no reason to get mad."

"So, you're really not together?" Jason asked hopefully.

"He wants to be, but we're not," Danny said, sounding cuter every second.

"Cool, but he's my friend and…"

"Nothing special, we'll just hang out like friends."

"Okay," Jason consented.

"When can you be here?" Danny asked, hoping for the best.

"A little bit later," Jason said.

"Okay, well, call before you come."

"Alright, see you then," Jason said, hating that this conversation was coming to an end.

"Alright, bye."

"Bye," Jason said, hanging up the phone. A squeal quickly followed, and Jason began punching the air in excitement. Snickers, who had just jumped up on the bed, quickly jumped off. She turned to hiss and meow. Jason was so happy now that he knew he was going to see Danny again. He jumped in the shower and got dressed as best he could (which was considerably better than before.) He then darted up to Abby's house to see if she wanted to come.

The following two weeks were taken up with going to Josh's apartment. Sometimes Jason brought Abby. Other times it was nice to be alone with just Danny. This boy, who was only one year younger than Jason, had a likeness to him much past his age. The way he took care of himself was envious. He always made sure his goatee was perfectly shaped and his clothing fit perfectly. Danny was always found wearing a polo shirt, collar popped, and vintage jeans hugging his waist. The flip-flops he wore were brown and plain. They did, however, hug his feet and were well worn in. Jason had found himself wondering where his feet had taken him, and what trials and achievements those sandals had been through. It was funny the closeness to jealousy Jason held towards these sandals, knowing that they had been through more than Jason had with Danny.

The same argument had continued between Josh and Danny for these two weeks. Josh was always insisting that they were together. Danny, on the other hand, had pushed this allegation away, claiming it was false. That last Friday night was when Josh finally said that Danny won. This final establishment of realization on Josh's part did not go without a sacrifice on Danny's. Josh decided that if they weren't together Danny was going to have to move.

"Can I move in with you?" Danny had asked Jason.

"No, my mom would not allow it," Jason responded unhappily.

"Can you just ask her for me?"

"I can try, but I can't promise you anything."

"Just check, can you?" Danny asked with his eyes pleading as hard as his lips. Jason would love to have Danny come and live with him. Danny and Jason had expressed their lust towards each other already. There was no explaining the artistic and pure euphoric way this lust was explained. Jason liked it, and he only hoped Danny did as well.

Chapter 14

Danny moved home with his mother for a while before he moved back in with his ex-boyfriend of eight months. Jason hadn't talked much to him once he moved back. Danny hadn't had the time. Jason thought a lot about him while he sat there behind his cubicle. A phone call would come in, and Jason worked the call over as if he had been doing this his whole life. When the phone call ended, there were still thoughts of Danny.

This continued for weeks while Danny only called a few times. When Jason would answer these calls a smile quickly spread across his face. Talking to Danny made Jason happy. They seemed to just talk and talk about anything. Jason, keeping up his flirtatious side, always said something cute. Both would laugh and go onto the next subject.

The girls at work always knew when Jason had talked to Danny. The smile that would not wipe away was their first clue. He would then become very enthusiastic about his work, and would take more calls than any of them. Jason would tell the girls wonderful things about Danny. They would huddle around and listen to Jason's love stories.

Calling off of work one Tuesday was something Jason rarely did. He had been up all night, however, thinking about Danny. You see, the last day Jason saw Danny at Josh's house something had happened. Small as the gesture may have been, it made Jason very happy. Danny and Jason had done their aerobics with each other earlier, which kept them frisky the rest of the day. After Jason got up to leave, and Josh ran into the bathroom, Danny motioned for Jason. He leaned in and gave Danny a soft and beautiful goodbye kiss. Danny then took a plain silver ring off of his hand and gave it to Jason. Jason looked confused, but Josh broke the moment.

"Just give me a call tomorrow then," Josh said, coming around for a hug.

"Alright," Jason said, hugging him back and kissing his cheek, his fist still closed tightly around this ring.

Being a witch, Jason could sense Danny's slow, rhythmic, romantic energies vibrating vividly from this ring. The ride home Jason couldn't help but to turn the ring over and over in his hand. What was meant by Danny presenting this ring? *Don't bother trying to understand*, Jason had told himself, and slid the ring perfectly onto his left hand's thumb. Here it felt warm and natural. It rested securely between the knuckles. Jason was happy. Jason was truly happy.

This scene seemed to swarm around his head like a poison. He was lying in bed now, listening to his techno music. Jason only really liked beautifully remixed music from the radio, remade with a bumping techno beat. He also liked the awesome female vocals that sang about love. It was funny the way Jason was. He seemed to be one of the only people that truly understood love. Well, he believed so. He hated hearing stories of drama that were made into a story of love. "He hit me, but I won't leave him because I love him." Jason knew. He knew that this was not love. For some reason Jason felt that he knew what true love was like. It was more than could be explained in one sitting, so no one wanted to hear it.

The cell phone rang, but Jason did not recognize the number. He sat debating with himself. *I wonder what this person thinks is love?* Jason asked himself before answering the phone.

"Hey," the voice said.

"Danny?" asked Jason.

"Yeah, hey, what are you doing?" Danny asked, sniffling into the phone.

"Why…what's wrong?" Jason asked, determined to find out.

"Nothing, well, he's kicking me out…*sniff*…and I have nowhere to go."

"Aww."

"I have been crying all day." Then more to himself, "I'm such a mess."

"I'm coming up there."

"Did you ask your mom yet?" Danny asked.

"No, but I will ask her."

"Okay, and come up, no one is here."

"Alright, I'll call her now."

"What?"

"I'll call my mom now," Jason reiterated.

"'Kay, bye."

"Bye." Jason immediately called his mother at work.

"Hey Mom?"

"What!?" she asked, apparently irritated.

"You know that verse in the Bible, something like, 'I was hungry and you gave me nothing to eat. I was tired, and you gave me nowhere to sleep. I was naked, and you gave me no clothes.'"

"Yeah, what about it?"

"Well then someone asks, 'But lord, you have never been hungry, tired, or naked.' But then Jesus said. 'If you did it not to the least of these, you did it not to me.'"

"Yeah, very good Jason, are you reading your Bible again?"

"Yup," Jason lied. "But my good friend is getting kicked out of his house and he has nowhere else to go." Jason buckled his seatbelt, and started the car. "So I wanted to know if he could stay with us for a few weeks, till he gets his feet on the ground?"

"I don't know…I have to think about it," His mother said.

"Alright, but remember, 'If you did it not to the least…'"

"Yeah, I know Jason, keep studying that Bible."

"Okay, love you."

"Love you too," she said before Jason hung up the phone. He was at the main stoplight now before he makes a right to go up by where Danny lived.

Almost there, Jason realized that he didn't know where Danny lived. He had to call Danny back at the number quick. The phone rang in his ear for what felt like forever. Danny finally picked up the phone. Jason stayed on the phone with him. He had to call him back a few times because reception kept failing out. Jason climbed the stairs with the climbing urge to just give Danny a great big hug to let him know he was really there for him. He knocked on the door, which was already cracked open.

"Come in," came Danny's voice from the corner of the softly lit room.

"Hey," Jason said, fighting off the smile that wanted to make a grand appearance. He knew this was not the time for smiles, no matter how happy he was to see him. Danny was hiding under a large maroon comforter. Hearing random tapping on a keyboard let Jason know he was on a laptop. He sat there waiting for Danny to come out of his shell. The room he sat in was painted by someone that was apparently very happy. It was a lively orange creamsicle color. It was defiantly an amateur's job. The ends were unsmooth and jagged. The once white, now smoke yellow chair rails stayed unpainted. The strong wafting smell of dog was annoying his nose when Danny popped out.

"Did you ask your mom?" he asked

"Yeah, she said she has to think about it."

"Oh god, she'll say no. My mom won't let me move back in with her, and neither will Josh." He trailed off now, looking at the light tan colored carpet. "I have nowhere to go." He quickly ducked back under the sheet and sniffles could be heard.

"She will probably say yes," Jason said to the lump of comforter. Danny's eyes then poked out from behind the lump.

"You think so?" Danny asked, more with his eyes of hope than with his mouth.

"Yeah."

"I hope so," Danny said, eyes becoming quickly glossy. "I'm sorry you have to see me like this."

"It's okay."

"I just don't know what to do." He began to cry. Jason reached his arm around and pulled him into a hug.

"We'll stay at my mom's for a while, and we'll get a place."

"You promise?" Danny asked, looking into his eyes.

"I promise," Jason said, knowing that when he made a promise he could not break it. Danny stopped talking on the computer and curled up tight by Jason. He just held him, and kept the promise in his mind. He was already making plans. He leaned back knowing, or hoping, all would be okay.

Chapter 15

Moving Danny into the attic was a joy for Jason. His mother had said that Danny could move in. They brought all of his stuff up and put it in the hallway. The two had begun a cleaning frenzy. It was early May, and so the windows were open as they cleaned. Jason worked for the makers of Lysol, so they had plenty of cleaning supplies on behalf of the company. The cleaning, the incense, and the scented candles began to make the room feel very cozy. The floor got a nice layer of Teflon, which made your feet glide along it.

The room was still under construction when they both needed a break. It was now evening and it was becoming a bit brisk. The windows remained cracked so that the fresh air wrapped around them. It was welcome like a cool blanket. Having bought a dresser, the boys began to put it together. "I wonder if that boy could help us," Danny said when they looked at the directions and their jaws dropped.

"What boy?" Jason asked.

"Your neighbor boy."

"Oh, Shane?" Jason asked.

"I dunno, if that's the hot one that was out there."

"Yeah, but he's straight."

"So, never stopped me before," Danny said chuckling.

Jason just smiled. *Did he actually say that? I thought he liked me? Maybe he's just making conversation.* Jason really wasn't sure. He just let it go out, like the candle in the window after a nice cool gust blew through it. The night lasted long with them talking and just having a plain good time. From outside the window you would have seen two young men enjoying the company of each other. You would have thought they had a lot of catching up to do. They just talked the night away, before they both said good night and closed their eyes. Jason went to sleep that night a bright beacon of happiness. His whole body seemed to float.

Jason was up the next morning with the sun. He was preparing for work, when he thought he should call off. He left the room making as little noise as he could. He made it to the cordless phone, but realized that he had to go to work or it would be a bad paycheck. He put the phone back feeling defeat. He continued to prepare for work, constantly glancing at Danny sleeping. It all seemed weird, how he only met Danny about a month ago, and now they were living together. Jason, knowing it was about time to leave, left a note for Danny. He sat back on his bed. Unsure as to what to write, he began with the basics.

Good morning Danny,

I had to leave for work, so you know my number if you need me. After 8:30 the house will be empty. The computer password is "Linda." We don't have long distance on the phone, so you can't make those calls. I showed you where the bathroom is. If you get hungry I left you seven dollars to get a drink and something to eat. There's a great café just down the street. I also left you a few cigarettes to help the time pass.

Cya,

Jason

He read over the note and was unhappy with it, but had no time to re-write it. He got four cigarettes out and placed them on top, then some money. He stood there for a moment taking in Danny's beauty. He really didn't want to go to work. He left the room and made the descent to his car.

Time traveled so slowly at work. He was unable to focus, and he got reprimanded for telling a lady that he personally would look into something. Danny had called but Jason couldn't talk long.

"Hey."

"Hey, call me back at two, I have lunch then."

"Okay, but Linda isn't working."

"Are you capitalizing the "L"?"

"Yeah," Danny responded, a small amount of stress in his voice.

"Well don't, call me at two."

"Okay."

Jason hated hanging up but he had to do his work. They talked at lunch the whole time. Jason was coming home at six. Kyle, Jason's brother, was the first home that day. He was surprised to see someone he didn't know sitting at the computer. Kyle hadn't been informed of anyone new living in the house. He was pissed, and called his mother screaming about someone else living there. Kyle scared Danny.

"He looks like a giant," he was telling him as Jason pulled up in front of this house.

"Aww, I'm sorry," Jason said slamming his door shut.

"Where are you?" Danny asked.

"Home."

"Really? Good, I'll see you when you get in," Danny said with a newfound enthusiasm. Jason went inside and both galloped upstairs to the attic. There Danny flopped onto his air mattress and Jason lit a cigarette. Jason began to change out of his formal wear and slid into comfortable jeans and a button-up shirt. Jason's hair was longer now, so instead of spiking it he waved it, so the hair came out onto his face. It gave him a nice sort of "I don't care" look. It was obviously planned. Jason's eyes gleamed today with happiness. He put on the radio for some background music and continued to talk with Danny.

The music was now becoming a nuisance so Jason turned it down low. The conversation had turned to what had happened with his ex. Jason just wanted to know why he was kicked out.

"He's psycho, and he made me feel crazy," Danny said playing with the hem of the comforter. "I actually tried killing myself once because of him."

"What? Why?" Jason asked, now concerned.

"Well, he just always made me feel like shit, and so one day I took a whole bottle of Xanax It was the worst feeling in the world. I lay in bed, and douche bag walks in and sits on the computer. He was saying stuff to me but I couldn't understand. I just rolled over and fell off the bed. I don't remember what happened after that." There was silence. "I don't know what possessed me to try to kill myself over him."

"Oh my god, Danny," Jason said, now dropping everything he had been doing. "No matter what, you are more valuable than anything he could ever want. Why take your life when it's someone else that is making you feel that way? God, people like him should be killed just for being rotten lowlifes. Eww, and that probably made him feel like he had full power over you."

"Yeah, cuz after that everything was just ridiculous. He kept saying shit like, 'Oh, why don't you try killing yourself again,'" Danny said, now sounding more monotone than ever. Jason knew this dark place. He had gotten close enough to suicide when he became scared. It is a deep, dark, complex, and scary place. Jason needn't hear anymore.

"Well, he's a retard, and the next time I see him he will hear my mouth!" Jason exclaimed, feeling tension rise up from nowhere. "Let's go see what Abby's doing," Jason suggested, rising off of the bed. The sun had gone down since they began talking. The sky was now a dark blue with the promise of a dark night. Both got ready, but Danny took a few minutes longer. He went through a ritual of changing clothes to find the right outfit. He then sprayed a delicious cologne on him, which reminded Jason of passionate times spent. He eyed Danny with a peculiar interest and almost a yearning. Jason still in some sort of way felt jealous of Danny's flip-flops. He wanted to learn as much as he could about him. He found this young man to be extremely intriguing.

Danny looked up and caught his eye. Both stared into each other's eyes for a second. Both knew what they wanted, and they might as well have said it out loud the way they looked at each other. They broke eye contact and proceeded out of the house and up two houses to Abby's.

She opened the door with a great excitement, and the two were greeted with a loud, high pitched greeting. They walked in and went directly to the kitchen. "You guys wanna smoke a blunt?" she asked.

Both boys responded in unison, "Hell yeah!"

"Alright, shit, then we'll hit a cruise," she said.

"That's fine by me," Jason said, looking forward to this.

They went out to the car and made a stop at the gas station. Here Abby got out and bought a cigar. Jason then drove them up into the boondocks for them to roll up the blunt. It always took a little while before the thing was rolled. Abby asking for a lighter was Jason's clue that it was ready.

The conversation was normal for the first round, and part of the second. Then conversations turned into tangents with nonsense twists and ridiculous endings. Laughter followed, as everyone had successfully smoked themselves silly. Jason started to laugh really hard, but stopped when no one else was laughing. Collecting himself, he said, "I don't know what that was about."

A tangent of laughter quickly followed this statement. Jason caught Danny's eyes just then. Jason was caught in the moment. For some reason at that time Jason felt as if his heart grew wings and flew from his body. He wasn't sure where it went, but he was sure it was with Danny.

Jason had a romantic plan now brewing in his mind. He would take them up to the Indian tower. He envisioned him and Danny up top, huddled close and kissing with the city lights behind them. He turned up the road with this wonderful thought still floating through his mind. You see, Jason was just like any romantic guy, whether he is straight or gay. Instead of thinking girls to be romantic with, he thought of guys. He couldn't imagine it any other way.

"Yo, there better not be any cops up here," Abby said.

"Don't worry, me friend, there are none," Jason confirmed to her. They drove up to the top of this hill and Jason was right. Seeing no police around they all got out and ventured to this tower.

"Wow!" Danny exclaimed. "You can see everything from up here."

"Yeah, but you can see more from the top," Jason said. They all made their way up this spiraling staircase to reach the top. They all walked around the upstairs admiring the view. Jason now realized a problem. Abby wasn't in his daydream, and he was getting cold feet. The feeling Jason had felt was still there, but he had to act as natural as Danny was acting.

Jason's disappointment at realizing nothing was going to happen lead to his anxiousness of now wanting to leave. Abby left to go to her house, and Danny and Jason made it back to theirs laughing hysterically. They only made it to the attic hallway when Jason grabbed Danny's shirt and leaned in. They started making out and everything started happening rapidly. The breathing was louder when they wrestled their way into the room. Neither reached for the light, but Jason was sure to lock the door. The next hour and half that ensued was filled with pure bliss that Aphrodite herself would have envied.

The following weeks took shape in very much the same fashion. Jason would wake up early and leave Danny a note with some money. Work all day, and Jason would be back by six-thirty. The two would not participate in late night fiascos together anymore. Jason wanted more things to happen, but Danny was always tired. This behavior had actually gotten Jason to think a little. The blindfold of love was coming loose and he was starting to see things the way the were. That was the night Jason decided it was time to ask Danny a few questions.

"Hey, how was your day?" Jason asked, coming in from work.

"Boring, I smoked with your sister and brother though."

"Kyle and Melissa?" Jason asked.

"Yup."

"Whoa, I wouldn't do that because Melissa has a big mouth."

"She's not gonna say anything. She smoked too."

"Yeah, but she might always use that against you."

"Well, she won't. Eww, why are you like that?"

"Like what?"

"Judging your sister and stuff."

"Dude, she's my sister, I know her and I'm not judging her."

"Yeah, whatever"

"Yeah…whatever, Danny," Jason said, a little irritated at this point.

"I talked to this boy, and I'm probably going to the movies with him."

"Oh, that why your getting all dressed up?"

"Yup."

"Well, that answers a pressing question."

"What do you mean?"

"Nothing, I just wanted to ask you like what was going on between us."

"Nothing's going on, we're friends."

"Yeah, that's what I was afraid of," Jason said, lighting a cigarette.

"What do you mean? I never said we were dating."

"Yeah, I know, but the way we acted for a while…."

"What about it?" Danny asked, looking into the mirror and tugging at his waistline.

"Nothing," Jason said, really pissed off now.

"Well, I'm going now," Danny said, finally turning to look at Jason. "Are you gonna say bye, or are you still bitching?"

"Whatever," Jason said and turned onto his pillow, wanting to cry.

"Bye then," Danny said, walking out of the room and slamming the door. Jason lay there in the dimly lit room, his face in his pillow, crying. He had been so happy, just thinking that he had someone special. He liked coming home to a person that he really liked, instead of Snickers. She at that moment jumped up on the bed with a soft meow. She made her way up to the head of the bed and let out a crackled meow. Jason reached up and began petting her. He began to cry harder.

"Baby, all I want to do is love someone," he confessed, thinking on this wonderful concept. "Someone I really care for. What is wrong with me that nobody loves me?" He shoved his face back into the pillow and fell to sleep shortly there after.

Waking up around midnight to the bedroom door opening, Jason watched Danny walk in. The atmosphere seemed to not have changed. Jason, however, was now thinking rapidly. Should he show that he was hurt by this revelation of Danny's, or should he act like nothing had happened? Jason hoped that maybe Danny would realize how much it meant to him if he let the hurt show through.

"Why do you have the light on?" Danny asked, almost in an irritated tone.

"Because I fell asleep," Jason responded, unsure of how to pursue things, but figured he should try. "How was your night then?"

"Oh, first you're pissed, now you want to know how it went?"

"I'll take that as a crappy."

"You wish it was. It was great, actually, we went to the Indian tower." But Jason had heard enough. He didn't want to hear about Danny making out with someone else. "We made out."

"Great..."Jason made sure this sounded forced. "You suck his dick too?"

"Fuck you, you fuckin' asshole."

"What, just asking, I don't know if that's what you do with all of your new friends."

"Whatever," Danny said before storming out of the room. Jason again began crying because he realized that he went about that the wrong way. He let jealousy take over, and it turned ugly. He would never say something as messed up as he just had. He really ruined it now. He stayed up until two in the morning. He then decided to go downstairs and apologize.

He walked down the noisy stairs. He noticed the change in temperature as he journeyed down the attic stairway. Taking a big breath, he opened the door. He was greeted with the smell of the cat boxes. That moonlight that was shining through the window was enough light to navigate. The downstairs light was on, so he began his descent. Stepping down the stairs he began to work on his apology. Through the kitchen he walked, and into the computer room. Clutter was piled on the table and desk as usual. No entity was in the computer chair. Jason checked the rest of the house and there was no Danny. He had realized that he really did it this time. He probably hurt Danny as much as he was hurt. Jason returned to bed and turned out the light. He again cried to sleep, but this time, it was because he hurt Danny.

He awoke again at three-thirty in the morning. He looked up and saw it was Danny. He didn't bother to turn on the light. Jason could still see him in the moonlit room undress and then quickly climb under his big comforter. "I'm sorry for earlier," Jason said to Danny. He might as well have said it to the darkness where it would get lost and be unheard. Danny never responded, but Jason didn't say anything further. He just turned over in his bed.

"Good night," Danny mumbled.

"Good night," Jason responded. If he had had tears to cry he would have. Instead he fell asleep with a sinking feeling in his gut.

Danny called Jason at exactly two the next afternoon, after Jason had finally decided on a chicken sandwich from the vending machine.

"Hey, I'm gonna be leaving to go with my ex for a little while, but I should be back by the time you get home," Danny said. Jason's face beamed with a smile at the apparent normalness now. He was, however, worried, thinking he was really going with his ex. Because of this insufficient being, Danny had attempted suicide three times, and he was continuously putting Danny down.

"You're going with your ex?" Jason had to confirm.

"Yeah."

"Well, sorry for last night," he said, but the message got lost somewhere in the wires. There was no response. "Have fun then."

"Alright, see you when you get home."

"Okay, bye."

Jason had at this point mixed emotions. He was happy at the apparent normalness, but was disappointed with Danny's unwillingness to respond to his apologies. *I wish I hadn't said that. He hates me now. No, he still likes you. Why did you say that? He wouldn't have called you if he hates you. Get your sandwich.*

Jason got his sandwich and ate it in silence. It was only a matter of time before he was clocking out and rushing to his car. Over the drive home Jason blasted his techno music and smoked cigarettes. By the time he had made it home he was in a great mood. Soaring up the stairs he reached the attic in almost record time.

Opening the door to his room, he was mildly surprised to see that Danny was actually there. He was, however, completely under his maroon comforter. "Danny?" Jason waited but there was no response. "Danny?" he tried again, stepping closer to the bed.

"What?" Danny asked with a crackling voice, followed by a sniffle.

"What's wrong?" Jason asked now, taking a seat at the bottom of his bed.

"Nothing." Sniffle, sniffle.

"Danny, you know you can tell me," Jason said, Danny didn't respond. Jason's eyes glanced around quickly for a pill container or a sharp blade. He then scanned once more for something that might be upsetting to Danny. Finding nothing and still not receiving an answer, Jason got up to leave.

"Wait...lay with me," Danny said.

"What?"

"Lay with me," he repeated. Jason slowly walked towards the bed confused. He wouldn't normally "lay" in bed with one of his friends. Jason would sit while they lay and talked. Feeling sorry though, he made his way under the covers.

"He told me that he has gonorrhea," Danny cried, letting the tears drop onto the pillow.

"He has what?" Jason asked, now scared himself.

"I know, he says I'm the only one he's been with," Danny continued to cry.

"Oh my God, Danny, you have gonorrhea and you didn't tell me!" Jason said, his voice sharp.

"No! I don't have gonorrhea. Well, I don't know."

"Oh my God! You never got tested?"

"Once."

"How long ago?"

"A year," Danny said. This was not settling well with Jason. He could not help racking his brain trying to remember symptoms of gonorrhea. He couldn't think of any except discoloration and painful urination.

"It doesn't hurt when you piss, does it?"

"No."

"You don't have funky stuff coming out, do you?"

"No."

Well, I think even if you do have gonorrhea there is a cure for both of us," Jason said, attempting to trick himself into security.

"Really?" Danny asked, wiping tears away.

"I think so," Jason replied. Danny turned away, and Jason held him close, putting an arm around him. "I'll call off tomorrow, and we'll go and get tested."

They stayed cuddled together for an hour before they went to smoke with Abby. They kept this to themselves and generally had a good night together. There were some instances where both would go silent, and they would think about this terrible news. That night, before they went to sleep, both exchanged a heart felt hug and kiss goodnight. Jason hardly got any sleep because Danny's sniffling remained constant.

Waking a little later than usual the next day, Jason stumbled out of bed. He didn't remember Danny coming to lie next to him, but there he was. He called his work to inform them that he was sick. His boss in her usual snootiness said. "Fine, see you tomorrow then," then she exhaled sharply and hung up the phone. Jason rolled his eyes and continued getting dressed.

He did not write Danny a note, because he was remaining home. He went to the kitchen and poured himself a glass of milk. He then began to search through clutter at an attempt to find the phone book. After looking through what looked like a dump site he gave up. He called information on the phone. "What listing?" asked the computer.

"Planned Parenthood," Jason annunciated carefully into the receiver.

"I'm sorry, please hold and an operator will assist you." Elevator music ensued before an actual person answered the phone.

"What listing was that?"

"Planned Parenthood."

"Alright, I'll connect you," the young man said. There was a click and then it began to ring. Jason made an appointment for eleven-thirty that morning. Realizing that Danny didn't usually wake until this time, Jason made a trip for breakfast.

His plan worked on getting Danny up. He smiled and gave Danny his steak, egg, and cheese bagel. "I got you some breakfast."

"I hardly slept."

"Me neither."

"Thank you," Danny said, taking the sandwich. "Why did you get breakfast?"

"Because we have an appointment for eleven-thirty at Planned Parenthood," Jason said.

"Eleven-thirty? So I can't go back to sleep after this?"

"Well you can, but we have to leave here at eleven."

"Okay," Danny said, taking a bite from his sandwich. Jason wanted to stay upstairs but figured he might as well check his e-mail. While he was at it, he paid his insurance bill and phone bill. Before he knew it, it was well time to wake Danny up.

Jason discovered that Danny had never gone back to sleep. He was instead up, dressed, and cleaning the room. The boys climbed into the car and set upon a journey to discover the unknown.

"I hope we don't have a guy checkin' our dicks," Danny said laughing.

"A gay guy," Jason laughed.

"A gay cute guy," Danny retorted.

"Yup, cuz then I would have a problem," cackled Jason.

"Or, he might just lose an eye," Danny said back, laughing. They both continued to crack jokes until they got there. They were still laughing when they walked in. Jason walked over to the registration desk and signed them in.

The testing was free, but it was painful. Both had blood taken and about three cotton swabs stuck into their urethras. They were both unhappy to find out it would take twenty-four hours to get all of the results back. They got checked for every STD just to make sure.

Both walked from Planned Parenthood now more scared than ever. The jokes did not continue in the car, and hardly a word was spoken to each other all day. It was very awkward and disturbing silence. Abby had even picked up on their silence and asked what was wrong. Neither replied.

That night before bed, they only had a short conversation. "I hope everything's okay," Danny said, pulling his comforter up snug. Jason, immediately behind him, responded.

"Me too." He then pulled his side of the covers up and held Danny close. "Good night."

"Good night."

Chapter 16

Warm and snug, they took their time waking up the next morning. It was a disturbed sleep, but it was good. It was now eleven-twenty, so they knew the results should be in. Jason had woken at eight and called off of work again. Now his boss seemed even more snotty than ever. Jason ended his phone call with her, realized how much he hated her, and fell back to sleep.

"Do you wanna call?" Danny asked Jason. He had picked up his cell phone, and Danny leaned over his back.

"Yeah, might as well," Jason said, looking for the number. "Do you remember the password?" Jason asked.

"Was it spishnack?" Danny asked.

"No, it was smithrack," Jason responded, unsure himself. He dialed.

"Thank you for calling Planned Parenthood, this is Alyssa speaking, how may I help you?"

"Yes, me and my friend Danny were in yesterday, and we were told to call today to get the results."

"Okay, I'll transfer you to the lab; do you remember your counselor's name?"

"I think it was Amy," Jason said, looking back at Danny. He confirmed with a simple nod of the head.

"One moment please," she said while blues music played in the background. After ten seconds, it picked up again.

"Hello, this is Amy. What's your password?"

"Smithrack," Jason said. "S-m-i-t-h-r-a-c-k"

"Thank you…Okay, Jason and Danny, correct?" she asked.

"Yes."

"Okay. Our files are a little incomplete, are you two domestic same sex partners?"

"Um, yeah," Jason said unsure, but it sounded good.

"Okay, you checked out okay, both of you," she said. Jason gave Danny the thumbs up. Danny then jumped up, and turned on his side.

"Alright, thank you," Jason said.

"Okay, and would you like to schedule a six-month follow-up?"

"Not at this time," Jason responded and hung up the phone. Danny was under the comforter again. Jason raised it with a big smile on his face. It was quickly wiped away when he saw tears in Danny's eyes.

"I was really scared," Danny cried.

"I was too, but we're happy now."

"These are tears of joy, are you kidding me?" Danny said with a smile on his face. That was the first time either had really thought hard about having an STD. They curled up together once more and fell back to sleep.

Two months had passed, now making it three months that they were living together. Everywhere Jason went, Danny went too. They had become inseparable. Affection only really came every once in a while, but Jason soaked it up when it did. Jason had come to terms with the fact that they were friends, and he loved it. He still wanted to be with Danny, but being his friend beat having nothing at all. Both now had a different vocabulary towards each other. They now said before going to sleep, "I love you." Jason truly meant it too. Even with suppressing his want to be with Danny on a romantic level, Jason knew he loved him. It was a complete understanding. When

Jason thought on it, he was happy. When Danny said it, it was like shivers all over. It was in the air, and it proved so true. It was almost tangible, even through the fights.

Jason had since taken several sick days now that it was July. The sweltering heat drew them all to the local swimming hole. Shane, the next door neighbor, had become a regular as well. Initially, Danny had tried to seduce him in any way, but nothing worked. They melded a weird little friendship group, and they did everything together. Everyone loved Jason and Danny. They had become the highlight of any social get together.

Swimming was the guys thing. Jason, Danny and Shane would go to the creek to go swimming. Shane's girlfriend came along, with Shane's cousin and her friend. The last two would just wade in, but the boys had more in mind than that. They would climb a tall tree that went over the creek and would jump in. Jason was scared the first time, and it seemed like a lifetime before he actually jumped. He seemed to fall forever, before he slammed into the murky waters. The water tasted gritty and bitter.

Everyone had cheered that he jumped off, and Jason put a fist in the air as an accomplishment. Little did he know how much of an accomplishment he had achieved. Not only did he jump off of the tree, but he jumped off of the insecurities. He jumped off the predictable ways. He jumped off the predestined Jason, and dove into a whole new world of thought.

He now loved the thrill, and could only race as fast as his now-slick shoes would let him. He climbed to the top with a new confidence. He jumped and did a front flip the same time Danny did. Shane waited at the top for the other two, for all three to jump off together. The water was starting to smell like cedar chips with fresh soil. He noticed that the water seemed a little colder now then it had before. Each time his body plummeted into the icy water, his breath was shocked away from him. He looked up and saw Danny and Shane jump in on either side of him, so he went under again. They came up, and Jason began splashing them. Danny swam over and dunked Jason. While he was under he pulled Danny's legs out front under him. Both came up laughing, and attacked Shane. He pushed them off, but slipped on the algae and fell in.

The guys were having a great time, while the girls sat either bitching or yelling at the boys. Now it has to be said that Shane was not gay. He did have a sensitive side, but that was as gay as he got. He was what some may call a "metrosexual." He dressed well, and had style like a gay man, but he was defiantly straight. Shane made a great friend because he understood a lot of the harassment and ignorance Jason and Danny got on a daily basis. Shane was weird about them being gay at first, but came to accept it. He treated them no differently than anyone else. In fact, he would come to them about things he wouldn't bother mention to his best friend. He just knew there would be good feedback from them. Because Shane was a metrosexual, and lived in this little town, he was often confused with a homosexual.

Jason had kept a copy of a newspaper article that had in someway changed his life. It was called "What's the Issue: Homosexual's Sin." Jason held on to it because it was that day when it hit home that he was gay. There was a list of things on "How to Spot a Homosexual." Shane had fit about nine of the ten things as well as Jason. It wasn't long before he endured the same sort of harassment Jason had gone through.

It was a hurtful bout of rumors and hazing, but both had survived. The worst antagonizer, both agreed, was Seth. He was relentless, and went through hell just to humiliate both guys. After Adrian's attack, everything only got worse. He was in News Production class the semester after Jason. It was then that the worst had happened. Seth had a small segment called "Car of the Day," where someone's car was featured each day. This day Jason saw his car. Seth walked up to the car with the microphone. "This is the gayest car, because it is driven by the gayest gay, Jason." At that moment Jason shrunk into his desk and wished he was invisible. "If you look at the back you see a rainbow. A nice flavor to some, but I did research. The rainbow is the gay flag. It's good to know Jason's proud. Signing off, Seth." Jason watched in fury. He did not have a rainbow on his car, and he was going to be even more pissed and file harassment charges if there was. Well luckily it had been a type of washable finger paint. When the principle went to get the tape, it had magically disappeared. Jason was furious.

That had passed now, and Jason forgave him for all of that when he saw something later. It was past. Nothing mattered now. The warm air swept over his body as he climbed out of the water. This seemed to help clear his mind. Just then Danny pantsed Shane. Shane's girlfriend screamed, and his cousin and friend yelped and looked away. Jason was surprised to see what the god had blessed him with, but did not want to look at Shane in this way. He laughed, and raced to the top of the tree.

They all played until they got hungry. Jason called in delivery for when they got home. They ate, and played video games very loudly. Shane's girlfriend left, and warned Jason and Danny that they couldn't touch Shane. Both began rubbing Shane's chest, since his shirt was off. She shrieked "Oh my God!" and came running into the room.

"Cock block," Danny coughed. All the guys laughed. His girlfriend smacked Danny on the arm.

"Bad Danny!" she said. "Jason get back!" she yelped as she caught Jason reaching for Shane. They all laughed and she gave up. She left, and the guys devoured some more pizza. Abby eventually came over, and they all smoked a fat blunt. It had been forever since Shane had smoked, but it made him laugh very hard, which caused him to drool. While Danny played the video game Jason gave Shane a back rub. The players switched up, and now Jason rubbed Danny's. Abby sat on the bed munching on chips before she started asking to take pictures.

"What?" Jason asked.

"When you guys all go at it, can I take pictures?" she asked. The guys just started laughing. Smoking pot seemed to make everything so much funnier.

"Yo, I just thought she finally lost it," Jason laughed. "I thought she was talking to herself."

"I thought she was talking about the video game," Shane chimed in, finding it hard to say through the laughter.

"No, I just think three guys going at it would be hot..." Abby confessed.

"Well, you won't see any of that," Shane spoke up.

"Damn!" Abby cursed at the ground, eating another chip. Jason and Shane exchanged looks and laughed under their breath. "Whatever, I'm leavin'," Abby said before storming out. "You faggots have fun."

"Get out, Hag," Danny yelled back in a playful voice. She just smiled and proceeded down the stairs. The room stayed silent for a while, only broken by Shane's flatulence.

The guys finished up the evening with a gruesome French horror movie. Jason had never felt more alive than he did today. He figured that this was what it was like for most boys on a daily occurrence. When the horror movie was over, and Jason nearly wet his pants, they put in a comedy. The boys laughed and continued to eat the old pizza every now and again. Once the comedy was over the boys sat back, now tired. They, however, had already planned out the entire Saturday ahead. Jason slept in the bed with Shane, while Danny lay on the couch. Shane didn't worry about Jason sleeping next to him, because he knew he was safe.

Shane was snoring, and Jason's eyes were closing when Danny jumped right in the middle. Shane woke with a start, and went to punch. Danny was quick and grabbed his arm. Jason then plowed into Danny's side knocking him off. These two wrestled, when Shane picked up pillows and began hitting both. Danny and Jason lunged at Shane, and knocked him backwards onto the bed. The guys roughhoused for about fifteen minutes before taking a two-minute break. Shane was the first to initiate round two. The second round only lasted ten minutes before Jason landed on Shane's thumb and bent it all the way back. A painful crack was heard as Shane adjusted it to normal again. He then wailed Jason with a golf ball in the back. It hurt, but Jason considered them even. They all laughed themselves to sleep, happy and content with a great day.

The next day began with a grand breakfast at the diner. This time it was on Shane. It was a boy's day out, and they all had a blast. They played laser tag, raised some ruckus at the mall, went swimming, made the movies, and annoyed the waitress at the nearby restaurant. They had all decided that they wanted to smoke, so they found Abby.

They decided to go to the wooded area at the park. They thought it would be fun to go for a walk in these woods in the middle of the night. It was a new moon tonight, just as Jason had read in his almanac first thing this morning. This being the case, the darkness threatened to be impenetrable

Armed with just the light from their cell phones they proceeded into the now misty woods. They stuck close and smoked the blunt before they were in the middle of the woods. Somehow, however, Shane had managed to get them off of the path. They didn't really know where they were. Information began to go through the fog the pot had caused in Jason's brain. He began to worry that they had been "Pixie led," he said out loud.

"What?" Everyone asked at the same time.

"We were pixie led off of the trail, where we become confused by a trick played on us by pixies."

"Oh god, here he goes with his witch shit," Danny muttered.

"No seriously. We should walk backwards, or turn our shirts around so they can't tell if we're coming or going."

"What the..."Shane began.

"I know," Danny said to Shane.

"Look, here's the path!" Abby yelled, pointing down now at the plain earth. "Talking about spirits and crap, don't do that!"

"Sorry, it was just a thought," Jason apologized, after apparently scaring Abby. They trudged along the path now led by Abby. Everyone knew where they were now, except for Danny. They walked up and then down. Jason warned everyone to stay right, because on the left was a steep ravine that led to a small shallow creek. Danny moved his phone to the left and saw what he was talking about. He also saw a thick rope hanging from a tree.

"Whoa, do people swing on this?" Danny asked.

"I guess so," Jason replied. They took only about three steps past the rope, when they all jumped. A piercing, and very loud wail was heard immediately behind them. Shane's light was the brightest, and they saw that the rope was now swinging violently. They all screamed, and literally ran out of the woods in sheer terror of what may be following. Jason was brave and remained behind the other three. He was busy keeping up his tower of light visualization his mentor in the craft had taught him. He strained not only to run, but to extend his energy to protect them all.

It was no wonder that Jason was the most out of breath when they got to his car. They scrambled to get inside. Jason became disoriented when a brilliant light shone on his car. It took him a second to realize that it was a cop. Now he began shaking, knowing that they should not have been there after sun down. Jason turned off his car and rolled down the window in anticipation of the officer.

The officer shone his light into the car, and then around the woods quick. He strode over to the car with a long, slow stride. He shone his flashlight in Jason's face, "License and registration," he said, now bending low and shining the light on everyone's face. "Abby, it's a wonder to find you at a disturbing the peace complaint," he said sarcastically.

"We meant nothing by coming…"Jason tried to say.

"Was I talking to you?"

"No, sir," Jason responded respectfully.

"What are you guys up to?" the officer asked, once again shining the light in everyone's eyes.

"We were trying to freak ourselves out," Abby said calmly.

"Well, did you succeed?" he asked. Everyone nodded their heads. "Why, what happened?" It was like he had just turned on four different televisions because everyone started talking at once. "Whoa, whoa, whoa…Well I guess you did, so you guys weren't drinking or doing any drugs?" he asked, shining the light directly at Abby.

"First night I've been sober actually," she lied.

"Thank you for your honesty, Abby," he said, handing Jason's license and registration back. "You kids get out of here, and don't let me catch you here again," he said, then walked away. He shined his light at the woods one last time and seemed to hold on an odd shadow before he got in his car and turned off the spot light. He drove off in a hurry and left the kids there.

Jason got a cold chill on his neck and knew they had company. He quickly turned over his engine and backed up. Looking into his rear view mirror he saw a shadow, tall and flowing, glide across the road and stop by the tree. It kept its two greenish glowing eyes especially on Jason. Terror filled him, and he looked away as quick as he could. He hoped he was freaking out because of the marijuana, but kept up the tower of light exercise anyway.

They got home and everyone went to Shane's house. Jason promised he would be over. He went straight to the other room next to his bedroom. This he liked to call his witch room. He kept his tools and dried herbs among other magical things in this room. He cleared his circle with his broom and lit the candles that were situated in the four cardinal directions. He brought salt, sage, and blessed moon water into the circle. He called to the four watchtowers and sat in the center circle. He took the athame and held it in his hands. He slowed his breathing and concentrated on tiny spider webs attached to his body. The then took the athame and cut those tiny webs. He then lit one black and one white candle in the center and sat in total concentration of negativity being vanquished. He picked up the athame with its silvery strands of webbing attached. He touched the tip to the black flame, and then touched it to the white. With a tiny string he tied the black and white candles together so their wax would mix. He sprinkled very little salt and very little sage into the water, after he sprinkled himself. This was to purify and protect him. He then drank the cold water, and felt a warming sensation fill his entire body. A smile spread across his face and he knew his countermeasure had worked. He would not blow out the candles in the quarters, as this showed disrespect to the elementals of fire. Instead he snuffed the flames, but left the black and white candles with their wax flowing together, burning.

He had returned to Shane's house. Abby had left, and Danny and Shane were playing video games. Jason stayed for a little, but found himself becoming distracted very easily. He returned to his room, and picked up, *To Have and Have Not* by Ernest Hemingway and began to read. He read straight through the book before Danny came back. It was now five in the morning. "I cuddled with Shane," he said excited.

"Yeah okay," Jason said, taking off his glasses and folding the arms. He put them down and rubbed his tired eyes.

"No, you don't understand. He was backing up into me," he said.

"So why the hell are you back here?" Jason asked. He was setting the thin cover on his bed, so he could get under.

"Because he said he had to deliver papers," Danny said. Jason laughed. He knew that Shane hadn't delivered newspapers in over a year. "Why are you laughing?" Danny asked.

"I dunno, that must suck," Jason smiled, now climbing into his thin pajamas. "I still don't believe you." Jason confessed.

"You don't have to."

"I know," Jason said. Danny crawled under his covers. Jason went over and gave him a hug, "Good night," he said.

"Good night."

Jason turned off the light and slipped under the covers. "I love you."

"I love you too," came Danny's voice. Jason was happy. He slept, and he was happy.

That Wednesday while Jason was at work he received a call. He bent low to answer so his boss wouldn't see him. Knowing it was Danny, he picked up.

"I am going with my mom to Ohio to visit family," Danny informed him

"When will you be back?"

"Saturday or Sunday."

"Saturday or Sunday!" Jason repeated. "Why so long?"

"It's only three days."

"Only three days!" Jason exclaimed, shocked. He couldn't believe there would be no Danny for three days.

"You can call me on my mom's cell; I'll leave it on your bed for you."

"Alright."

"So, I'm leaving in fifteen minutes."

"Okay."

"Alright, bye."

"Danny?"

"Yeah?"

"I'm gonna miss you."

"Don't, just call me."

"That doesn't work."

"Well, I am gonna miss you too," Danny said.

"Okay, well I love you, be safe, have fun, and I love you," Jason said,

Danny giggled. "I love you too," he said.

"Bye."

"Bye," Danny said and hung up the phone. Jason wanted to say bye or I love you just one more time. The consumer on the phone had, however, been on hold almost the whole time. Jason went to un-mute it, when the consumer hung up the phone.

Jason made it home sad as could be. He went upstairs to get the number to reach Danny. He called the number from his phone. No one picked up on the other end. He threw the phone to the bottom of the bed. The following three days were miserable. Jason stayed in his room and read books. He realized how much Danny really had grown on him these last couple of months.

As much as he wanted to put it aside, he knew that he was madly in love with Danny. It must be said that it did start out as an infatuation. That infatuation then quickly grew into happiness, which led to friendship, which led to Jason being willing to do anything for Danny. Jason had never said he would lay down his life for Danny. Knowing Jason as well as we do, we know he would do just about anything for anyone, so he may easily lay his life down for Danny's.

Jason knew it was love. When they fought, they were just

explaining their uniqueness in loud verbal statements. Neither ever said anything that would truly hurt the other. Jason found himself studying Danny in pure amazement. Time spent with Danny was his life. No other friend had such an impact on him. The true test was coming, but neither he nor Danny would know. Jason's tarot readings always foretold of a terrible problem. He assumed it was financial, and began taking steps to stop that from happening. Little did either know of the rapidly upcoming changes.

Chapter 17

Danny came back that Saturday, and Jason had bought new cologne for him to wear. He had the cologne when they first met, but had since used it all. They were in the room for a good hour talking and laughing when Abby came in.

"Hey," she said stepping in, and allowing a young black man in after her.

"Hi," Jason said. He was eyeing up the newcomer in his room.

"This is Terrance," Abby said, and they all exchanged greetings.

"Oh man, this room is hoppin'," he said, noticing the quotes Danny had written on the wall. His reaction was understandable because this room was completely re-done, while the rest of the attic looked like just an attic.

"You guys wanna smoke?" Terrance asked, holding up a large bag of the green stuff. Danny and Jason made eye contact, smiled, then both nodded. Terrance rolled the cigar very carefully, as if it were an art. They all talked and smoked, and Jason put on some music. Terrance seemed to like all the same songs as Jason, and they talked easily.

The smoke had not all cleared before Melissa surprised them all with her presence. "What are you guys doing?" she asked walking in and closing the door. She sniffed the air. "Oh, I know," she said, looking at Jason. Jason, being her big brother, did not really want her in his room, especially after smoking a blunt.

"Mel, go downstairs," Jason said.

"No, who's this?" she asked, looking at Terrance. "You're gonna be mad rude and not introduce me to this nigga?" she said to Jason.

"Yo, wussup, they call me 'T,' short for Terrance," he said, pounding his chest once with his closed fist. Terrance or "T" was a thug. He came from the nearby city. Melissa did not go away; instead she hung around like a fly on a warm summer's day. It was obvious to Jason that Melissa had a crush on this Terrance kid. Jason, however, knew that this kid was twenty years old. Melissa was only fifteen. Jason knew he could never have Terrance around if he didn't want her around as well.

She continued to hang around and talk, quite frankly getting on Jason's nerves by now. By the closing of the evening Terrance and Melissa seemed to be getting comfortable. This made Jason very uncomfortable.

It was no surprise to Jason the next day when Mary announced to him that Terrance and she were dating. He had slept over that night, which only added to Jason's discomfort. Dylene, Jason's mother, seemed to enjoy Terrance's company.

It was only day two and Jason was getting annoyed heavily by this newcomer. He was completely different in front of different people. Only a few hours around him was enough time for Jason to get annoyed. By day three, Abby had told Jason that Terrance was a crack head. Jason had taken that with a grain of salt, until Jason walked in on it at a friend's house. Later that night, after Jason came home from getting a drink for Danny, Terrance was waiting.

"Jason, I've got a question for ya," Terrance said. He seemed relaxed sitting on the front porch.

"What's that?" Jason asked, fumbling for the house keys.

"Do you think you could run me to the city?"

"For what?"

"You know the candy rock, rock, crack," he said, now seeming to get excited. "I have a five hundred dollar supply that just came in."

Jason couldn't believe what he was hearing. Was Terrance seriously asking him to get crack for him? *What is he thinking, he's dating my sister and he thinks he's gonna do drugs all like that?* "I would, but it's two in the morning and I have to go to work tomorrow."

"Oh okay," Terrance said, looking down.

The next morning before leaving for work he called Dylene at work. He informed her of what Abby said, walking in on him, and Terrance asking last night for that favor. She said she would talk to him. The only reason Jason voiced these concerns was because it was becoming apparent to him that he was trying to move in.

She never did talk to Terrance and two months had passed by. By now Terrance had never left the house. He was calling Dylene "Mom," and he got everything he asked for. Melissa had told Terrance that Jason thought he was a crack head. Jason wasn't alone, as Danny had walked in on him and knew he was too. The boys had put a padlock on the door for when they were away. They knew that crack heads would often steal just for a fix. Jason and Danny did not get along very well with Terrance. They just all seemed to clash.

Danny and Jason were closer than ever. Danny had finally gotten rid of those old worn-in sandals, and wore the new ones Jason had bought him. Jason was always spoiling that special someone in his life. He had accepted that Danny wanted to be friends. It was better now because they were best friends. You would hardly ever see the one without the other. When they said "I love you" it was trued and unaltered. Jason always made sure he was careful with saying to word love to people. If he felt like he wanted to say it, he would sit, meditate, and think on it a while. He only ever had to do this twice. Jayden and Danny were the only two he had ever thought about. He almost was there with Adrian, but he was the past now.

It had been a good day so far. Jason and Danny were planning to go to the mall. Jason had gotten a credit card and they found it was about time for him to get a new outfit. Jason had been consistently dropping the pounds due to his new exercise binge and watching his food. The boys were about done when Danny went for his cologne. It wasn't there. He gave Jason a look, which he returned. Danny checked every drawer, behind the dresser, under the bed, and in every nook and cranny in that room before he went downstairs to ask someone. The boys were pretty sure who would have taken it. They even asked Shane first. Danny was down right furious that the gift Jason got him was gone.

"Dylene, you wouldn't happen to know where my cologne is?" he asked as she was the first person he saw.

"No," she responded. He quickly changed gears and went down the stairs.

"Terrance, you know who took my cologne?" Danny asked.

"No," he said, faking surprise.

"Yeah, I bet you don't," Danny said, staring him down.

"What the fuck does that mean?" Terrance said louder, and standing up.

"Don't even stand up like you ain't got no damned sense," Jason said stepping foot in front of Danny.

"No, if he wants to come at me, let him," Danny said, gently getting Jason out of the way.

"I wasn't, but you say it like that, and I will come at you," Terrance said, now coming around the table. Melissa came in the room.

"Stop it, guys!" she screamed. Now Dylene came down the stairs.

"Shut the hell up, and sit the fuck down!" Jason said to Terrance.

"You wanna come at me too?" Terrance said to Jason. "Come on, I'll take both you faggots!" he yelled

That was what set them off. Danny came in with a hook, and Jason plowed him over. Both were surprised how quickly he got up. He came at Jason. The girls began to screaming and Dylene ran for the phone. Swinging on Jason, Danny came up behind and pulled his head back. Terrance turned and planted a fist in Danny's stomach. Jason, now purely enraged, grabbed Terrance's arms, pulled them back, ripped him, and begun wailing on his face. Turning and seeing his little sister crying was what broke the spell. Terrance began punching his chest and stomach when Jason gathered his fists and made him stop.

"Ah! I'm calling the police!" Dylene screamed, face red.

"Don't, we're done!" Jason yelled at her. He got off of Terrance and headed to the front door. Danny followed. Upon reaching the front door, Jason turned on a dime because he heard running. Terrance was coming at them again. Melissa ran after him and grabbed him. He then turned and cold clocked her on the side of the face.

Jason and Danny now ran at Terrance. Jason picked up a kinky glass vase and went to hit him with it. It was knocked out of his hands and landed softly in the wash hamper. Dylene screamed again and ran to call 9-1-1. The swinging fists quickly died away when Dylene came in screaming, "The cops are gonna be here!"

Danny wanted to leave, but Jason knew that it would be bad to leave. They instead sat on the porch smoking a cigarette. When the two police cars flew up on the house, they put the cigarettes out. The same cop that stopped them in the woods, along with a short and wide officer, came galloping over. "What's going on here?" the cop they knew asked. The boys told the story, and then the cop stopped them. He took one by one around the side of the house. Shane had come out with his girlfriend to watch the commotion. The officer seemed to like and try to scare Jason because he kept brining up jail and getting arrested.

Eventually the cops told them all to chill, told Terrance to go back where he came from, and everyone to have a good evening. Jason had told them that Terrance had hit Melissa, but she denied it, and blamed the welt on her falling. After the cops had left and everything was done, Jason knew there was still some heavy duty anger in the air. They went to the mall and tried to enjoy the rest of their evening.

When they got home, they realized that they had forgotten to lock the door to the attic. They rushed up the stairs, and began inspecting the room. There was nothing missing, but Danny had his cologne back. They hung out with Shane the rest of the night. He had just gone home when Dylene came up the stairs.

"Jason, Danny, I wanted to talk to you two," she said huffing, as she was out of breath from climbing the stairs. The boys just looked at each other, knowing it was going to be about the fight. "Listen, Jason, you have been doing nothing but trying to start trouble with Terrance."

"He's a loser!" Jason shouted in quick defense. "And a crack head!"

"He is not!" she said.

"Yeah, uh, he is. How are you gonna tell me, I walked in on him."

"Well I asked him about it, and he said he would never touch that stuff."

"Well, he lied right to your face."

"I want you two out," she said. "You have two weeks."

"Whatever," Jason said

"No, not whatever, two weeks."

"Bye," Jason said to her. She got up and opened the door. Then she turned. "I love y…"

"BYE!" Jason said a little louder and got up to close the door on her.

"God, I told you, you shouldn't have said anything," Danny started.

"And what? Just keep my mouth shut? I don't think so."

"Well now we're kicked out," Danny said.

"Not really, that bitch never backs anything up," Jason said, lighting a cigarette. "Besides, it would be nice to get out of this crack house." Snickers, sensing her dad's distress, came up on the bed. She crawled into his lap, and he began petting her.

"What are we gonna do now?"

"I don't know, I'll figure something out," Jason said. That is what he did all night long. Little did anyone know he was on his final warning at work because he had now missed over fifteen days. Knowing he was pulling it close, he decided it was well time to stop playing around. Even though Dylene hardly ever backed up what she said, Jason wanted to get out so he could really be himself.

Dylene kept on Jason through those two weeks. Jason would get annoyed because she would see Danny and Jason looking for apartments but she kept it up anyway.

That Friday Jason woke at nine o'clock to a banging on the door. He could hear a walkie talkie and he knew it was the police. Then again, Bang, Bang, Bang. "Hold on," Jason said, quickly throwing the bag of weed out the window.

"Okay boys, pack your bags and get out, or I have to arrest you," the officer said. With it being the same officer now three times running, Jason wasn't so scared.

"What!? She said September first," Jason said outraged.

"That's not what she just old me. She said you had two weeks three weeks ago."

"Okay, but I talked to her, and she said September first, God!" Jason said in mounting fury. "Where is she?"

"Downstairs," The officer answered.

"Can we go down there; I'd like to speak with her."

"Sure," the officer said, losing his intimidating side seeing it wasn't working.

"Why the hell are the cops here?" Jason asked Dylene.

"I told you two weeks," she said.

"Yeah, uh, but we talked and you said September first."

"Well, I changed my mind."

"Well, I gave you money."

"You gave her money?" the officer intervened

"Yeah, one hundred and fifty dollars for two friggin weeks."

"Okay, you said he isn't giving you anything and is threatening you," the officer said to Dylene.

"Threatening you!" Jason exclaimed

"Sir, I don't feel safe with them in my home."

"WHAT!" Jason said, and then laughed. "You're scared of your son?"

"Sir, see the way he mocks me?" she said to the officer. He just stood there and his head.

"That's pretty pathetic that you're scared of me."

"Alright! That's enough. Dylene, did you say two weeks or September first?" the officer yelled, finally getting fed up with this petty argument.

"The first," she said.

"Then you two work this out, I mean I have a community to serve," he said. "Is there anything else?"

"Why don't you ask her about the crack head that's living here?"

"A crack head?" he repeated.

"Yes sir, and did I mention he's twenty and he's having sex with my little fifteen-year-old sister?" Jason said.

"Officer, Jason's gay. I can offer help to a crack head, but Satan has got a strong hold of that boy, and I do not want this evil in my house," Dylene said, bluntly and coldly. Jason just looked at her in disbelief. Was that seriously what this was all about?

"Ma'am, I don't think Satan has anything to do with being gay. Like I said, sort this out. Jason, I'll see you tomorrow between four and six at the station. Bring your friend," the officer said before leaving. Jason and Dylene caught eyes for a second. He saw the hate in her eyes. She really thought he was possessed.

"So Dylene wants us out because we're gay," Jason said, walking in the room to Danny packing his bags. "And don't pack."

"I want to, but why?"

"Because we're gay."

"Nu-uh!

"Yup, that's what she told the officer," Jason explained.

"Wow, that's really messed up," Danny said, getting a very disgusted look on his face.

"Tell me about it." That was what he said before he looked at the clock. It was ten-nineteen. His breath was sucked right out of him. He had not gone to work, nor did he call. He ran down the stairs and called. They told him not to come to work, but to pick his stuff up on Monday. This was a pay week, so he had to wait until Monday now to get it.

With this news Jason began to cry when he got to his room. He was going to lose Danny, his home, his job. Everything he had was now gone. How could this be happening?

"What's wrong?" Danny asked, putting an arm around him and laying over him.

"I lost my job," Jason said into the pillow

"Did you just say you lost your job?" Danny asked. Jason just nodded. "Are you kidding! What are we gonna do now?" Danny asked.

"I don't know," Jason cried. He was scared. He didn't want to lose Danny. He truly loved him. Danny cried over Jason, and they lay there until the sun went down. They then ventured over to Abby's to smoke and try to have a good rest of the day. He wasn't really looking forward to the police officer tomorrow either. They told Abby everything that happened. She then seemed to be dead set on killing Dylene.

The next day Jason and Danny sat plotting how they were going to get through this. Danny came up with some ideas but none came through. Jason had some people offer for him to stay, but he refused them. He had promised Danny that they would stay together. Four o'clock came around the corner before they came up with any type of a plan. They ventured down to the police station to talk with the officer. It was a warm, dry day so they walked.

They were buzzed through door after door. "Ah, gentlemen, take a seat," said the officer, whom they could call Officer Kelper. "Do you guys know why you're here today?"

"No," they responded in unison. They weren't sure if they should be comforted or scared by the smile that appeared on his face.

"Jason, you said that Dylene has a crack head living there?"

"Oh, yeah. She does," Jason said.

"And Danny, you know this too?" Officer Kelper asked.

"Yup, and there's plenty more," Danny said, as the hatred came to the surface.

"Okay, Danny, wait outside in the chair."

"Alright," Danny said, turning on his heels.

"Jason, have a seat. Now I am going to document this. This is a willing testimony, but you do not have to answer any questions unless you want to. Do you understand?" Officer Kelper asked.

"Yes, sir."

"Great, then tell me everything." Officer Kelper's pen didn't stop moving for quite some time. Jason put everything out on the table. He told him everything he said at the house and then some. Dylene had turned into something different. It wasn't his mother. Maybe it was, but it took him eighteen years to see her true side.

Danny then gave his story, which seemed to take quite a while. This made Jason wonder if Danny knew more than him. No, maybe he's just going deeper into detail. As he was thinking, Officer Kelper asked him to come back into the office.

"Now I believe that you boys are not the problem," he said, pouring some hot coffee. "Something is fishy about that situation, so I want you boys to do something for me."

"Okay," Jason said. Danny just sat in silence. Jason though he could see deep hurt, anger, and sadness in his eyes. In fact, they seemed to be watering a little.

"I want you boys to just get out of there."

"We can't. We don't have money."

"Well, there are some shelter's and crisis houses and things," Officer Kelper said, opening a drawer and presenting the boys with pamphlets.

"Okay, we'll look them over," Jason was saying as Kelper quickly interceded.

"Boys…I mean business. Get on with your lives, start dating each other, I dunno," he said. Jason and Danny both blushed. "Go on, get out of here," he said, waving his hand and leaning back into his leather chair. It made a crisp noise, compared to the hollow noise of the plastic chairs.

"Kay, that was weird," Danny said when they got outside

"Yeah, why'd he say that?" Jason asked.

"You probably told him to."

"No!" Jason exclaimed with a smile on his face.

"You know you want to date me," Danny said smiling.

"Can't deny that, but can't have that," Jason said, then turned to look at Danny over the top of his glasses. They exchanged smiles and walked home.

Chapter 18

A week had passed and the boys packed their bags. Danny had found a place to go at his sister's house, about an hour away. Jason had to move in with Shelley. They sat on the bed after their bags were in the car. They sat and stared at the wall for a second.

"Danny…" Jason began, feeling a tightening in his throat.

"Yeah," he replied with a crackling voice.

"You know I'm gonna miss you, right?" Jason asked with a tear falling down his cheek.

"I'll miss you too," Danny said, eyes watering.

"It's gonna be hard," Jason said, still stifling his tears.

"I know…" Danny said. Just then a horn beeped outside, and they knew it was his sister. "Well, I gotta go."

"Okay, I'll walk you down," Jason said, standing up and walking down the stairs.

"I love you," Danny said to Jason before opening the door. He pulled him into a hug.

"I love you too, Danny," Jason said, tears now falling down his face.

"I have your email address, so we can stay in touch."

"Okay."

"I love you."

"Love you too," Jason said before closing the door. Jason collapsed with sadness. The overwhelming giving up feeling closely hugged him. His heart beat rapidly as he lay there in a daze, knowing nothing more than to cry. He ran up to his room to be by Snickers. She lay there and listened to everything he said. He then scooped her up and carried her down to the car.

Jason no longer talked to Dylene. Life seemed to drag now. Danny was gone. He knew not if he would ever see him again. Jason hated to cry, but the thought of this drove him to even more tears. Depression and numbness was all that he felt anymore. Once again, he was alone. He felt like a burden to anyone who crossed him, especially to Shelley. He felt awful, not having a job and living there, knowing he didn't have money.

Shelley gave him money and she made breakfast each morning for him. His breakfast went untouched, his car cold from not being used. Jason wouldn't even get out a book. He lay there for a whole week, dead. He had no emotion, no will, no drive. He lost his hope and inspiration. He lost his love; no, the love was still there. He lost the one that he loved. He lost his joy, solace, and peace. He had lost everything that mattered, all because he was gay. Even to Shelley he was dead. She tried for weeks with no luck. For the first time in six years he felt that low, dark, scary place creep up on him again.

The day had come he decided he would go. He would drive to a wooded area. Here, he planned to take Shelley's butcher knife and cut the long way up his arm. The knife was in his car, and he was working on the letter to leave in his car. He was writing, "…*The only thing I have left in my life is my cat and me…*" That is when it hit him. Exactly, he still had him! He still had a basis for something to go with. For some reason something sparked inside of him. He might have lost everything in his life, but he was still here. If he were still here, there must be a reason. Logical thinking was coming back to him.

As he thought this and fought off the dark thoughts he gathered his clothing. He shaved before he showered and gazed at his now small body. He had not eaten for two weeks and it clearly showed the way his bones stuck out. It scared him. He got into the shower and felt it cleanse away his fear. Not all, but some, just enough to get him through this day.

He used his lotions, cologne, and hair gel to make himself look good. Shelley was at work serving tables. He saw the money come in from this so he would try restaurants. The first was unpromising, the second only seemed to employ older ladies, but the third had a nice feel. He completed the application and looked for some one to give it to. Jason hadn't known that Stitla's sister worked here. He met her a couple of times, and knew she knew him. She came over and said she would grab a manager. This extremely beautiful lady with black hair tied back in a perfect ponytail came walking over. She shook his hand and sat across from him.

"Do you have any experience?" she asked.

"No, but I would love to," Jason said, putting a smile on his face and turning on his charm.

"Well, Vanessa says you're energetic and fun, and would make a great addition to the team," she said.

"She said that, did she?" Jason asked with a smile as Vanessa winked at him.

"Yup, so when can you start?"

"The sooner the better."

"There is an opening tomorrow if you'd like."

"Sounds good," Jason said, now feeling that fire inside begin to smolder.

"Okay, wear normal clothes and we'll see you tomorrow at ten," she said, putting a matching smile on her beautiful face.

"Great, see you then," Jason said, shaking her hand once more and turned to walk out of the door. He was beaming when he got outside. This was a new life, a new beginning, and it didn't look too shabby. He wished Danny was there to join in the excitement, but went along to Shelley's work.

It was getting easier now for Jason to fit into this new skin he had received. He was eating. The fire was now burning inside of him. He was skinny, and rather toned. He was making new friends at work and he was comfortable once again. Thoughts still tore at him at night making it difficult, but the shower the next morning wiped it all away. Something was still, however, missing.

Work was going well, and he loved moving around. His metabolism spiked, and he was loving this new freshness. He was making money, which went into the bank, and he and Shelley were going out together and having a grand time. All was fine until Jason came home from work after a particularly lucrative evening. Shelley was at the kitchen table and appeared to have been crying.

"Do you wanna go out somewhere?" she asked, dry eyed.

"Umm, I guess. Are you okay?" he asked.

"Yeah, let's go," she said, followed by a sniffle. They drove in relative silence. Jason was sick of waiting. He knew she had bad news. He thought on it. What could it be? They made it to her mother's house in a small town up on top of a big hill. Her mother stood in the kitchen, trying to aimlessly make herself look busy. Shelley sat down and pulled an envelope from her pocket.

"You need to read this," she said, so Jason read it.

Shelley,

You are breaking your lease by having your friend stay with you. So either he leaves, or you both go by tonight. I will be forced to file an eviction notice first thing in the morning if not.

Signed,

Herb

P.S. The lease also says no cats!

"Okay, I'll just go then," Jason said, trying to think quickly.

"I'm so sorry," she said, her eyes beginning to water. "My mom says you could stay here for a week or two until you get a place," Shelley said, now with a tissue in her hand.

"No that's okay. I think I have somewhere to go," he lied.

"Are you sure?" she asked. Jason noticed that her mother stopped what she was doing to listen.

"Yeah...hey, don't worry and don't cry," Jason said, feeling badly that she was crying. His worst fear had now become a reality. He did turn out to be a burden on her.

Jason called Abby when he got back to see if he could stay there a while. She said he could so he went. He had never unpacked his things so it was an easy move. Jason wound up having a great night out with Abby. He only had about a fifteen-minute drive to think about the terrible situation he was in. The rest of the night was drinking, laughing, and having an all-out great time. Something was missing. Even with this something missing he had a great night.

Two months had passed with constant parties and regular trips to the club. Jason always hoped to see Danny there, but their paths never crossed. Instead he was grappling with the new looks that came his way. Jayden, Alexus, Josh, and other people he had known before were amazed by his transformation. He had lost a lot of weight, which wasn't healthy, but he looked good. He was never more popular with the guys. Cute guys, ugly guys, it made no difference. Drag queens were even checking him out and sending friends to talk to him. His answer was always the same, however. No matter how hot the guy was he would only exchange numbers. When it came down to it he always said no. It wasn't because he was scared or nervous. There was a reason for his lack of interest, and he was sure it was Danny.

Every single time after the club, no matter how many complements or numbers he received, he still thought about Danny. It had felt like forever. He hadn't even talked to his mother, whom Jason had on several occasions. Jason never felt the same towards anybody. He hadn't even felt like this over Adrian. He was sure he would never feel this way towards anybody ever again. He knew what this was. This was what it was like to be in love.

He didn't lust over Danny, nor did he base this love on his looks. Danny, in his own way, was always there for Jason. Thoughts like this were enough to make Jason cry, even on a good day. He felt whole around Danny. He was safe and secure. Little did either know that they were both thinking a like. Neither did they know that at this time their hearts beat together. Little did they know what lay ahead, and little did they know how in love they truly were.

"Good night, Danny," Jason said out the window and through the tears.

Only fifteen miles away did Danny say, "Good night, Jason."

And if you could have been in both places at the same time, you would have heard them both say, closely together, "I love you."

Chapter 19

Jason had gotten his food and was walking out of the café, when he noticed somebody squinting at him. He looked back, and he knew who it was instantaneously. He had come here with him once before, but he could not believe that he was back. "Danny! Oh my God, what are you doing here?" Jason asked in full surprise at ever seeing him again.

"Well I moved to the city with my boyfriend," Danny said, stirring his tea. "You look good!" Danny said, looking at Jason from head to toe.

"Thank you, you too," Jason said, feeling his cheeks turn red from smiling so hard. "Why didn't you call me when you left?" Jason asked and with that question Danny looked down at his plate and began turning over his macaroni salad.

"I never knew how to reach you," he confessed, taking a sip from his iced tea. "So I came to find you." He took another sip from his tea and said, "Do you want to go somewhere?"

"Okay, yeah, let's get out of here," Jason agreed, leading Danny to his car. Danny, despite the depressing conversation they had, kept looking over at Jason admiring him. The transformation that Jason had gone through was amazing. He went from fat, sloppy and low self-esteem, to a tone, neat, clean, suave, high self-esteem interesting person. He was satisfied with his look and felt really good about himself.

"What?" Jason asked, looking at Danny after noticing an exceptionally long stare.

"I just cannot get over the change; I couldn't even recognize you at the café," Danny said.

"Aww, thank you," was all that Jason could really say. After driving around for about an hour they got back to the café to drop Danny off at his car. Danny then turned around to face Jason.

"Do you wanna hang out with me tonight?" he asked, in his mature, slightly crackled, soft voice.

"Umm, yeah, might as well. Do you have any plans?" Jason asked, taking in every aspect of Danny.

"Well, I thought maybe we could go to a club or to your house."

"Why don't we do both?" Jason asked, with a sparkle in his eye that was never there before.

"If you want to, we could do that," Danny said, motioning for Jason to get into his car.

"Let me drop off my car up the street and get changed, or bring some clothes and I will be right out," Jason said, now being happier than he had ever been. Danny had finally made a return to him. Knowing that someone really cared that much about him was the greatest gift he could have ever received. This beat everything that he had been working so hard for. It beat having friends everywhere he looked, and being in shape with a nice body. This was truly the best reward for his patience that he could ever have received.

Danny went upstairs with Jason to get some clothes, and he stopped and held Snickers. "Hey you, did you miss me?" he asked her while she looked him in the eyes and meowed through a purr.

Now holding up a polo shirt to the pants he had picked out, Jason said, "You know I think about you every day?"

"I think of you too," Danny confessed. They smiled at each other, but Danny still had more on his mind. "I can't keep going with Dave."

"Why?"
"Because."
"Because why?"
"Ugh, I don't have feelings for him," he confessed.
"That sucks," Jason said.
"Yeah, what about you? Are there any boys?" he asked.
"Nope, none."
"Why?"
"I dunno."
"Why?"
"Because."
"Because why?" Danny asked, followed by a moment of silence.

Jason looked down and began to spin his thumb ring. Jason looked at his ring, and felt the fire surge up inside of him. He remembered that day about a year ago when Danny had given it to him. He stepped closer to say this softly.

"Because I love you."

When Danny looked up at Jason, he realized how close he was to Danny's face. He just stared into his eyes for a minute, noticing the extra sparkle that had appeared, before he slowly went in for a kiss. It started out with a few quick pecks and then the two began to really kiss. This scene was most awkward, however, as both of them began to cry. Jason was crying because he was the happiest he had ever been in his life, and he knew that Danny really did love him. Danny was crying because he felt truly happy with Jason, and knew he would never want to leave his side again.

When the kissing had subsided the sun was setting. Neither of the boys had noticed what was going on outside of their little world. Jason quickly got up in complete disbelief at what had just happened, but walked back to his belts to finish his outfit. He had finally chosen an outfit when the two left to go to Danny's apartment. The trip to Danny's was mainly quiet except for the occasional, "I can't believe this is happening."

Danny lived in the south side of the city, which was cheaper living, but his apartment was rather nice. When you walked in the front door there was a small walkway decorated with a bundle of eucalyptus plant above the doorway ahead, and sconces on either side of the wall with corresponding colors. The whole entire apartment was decorated and was very clean, with nice modern furniture. Every surface that was open was decorated with flowers and other little trinkets. "Did you decorate this place by yourself?" Jason asked, while looking at an exquisitely difficult display of candles and seashells he recognized as the one he had at his house.

"Yeah, I did, actually. It wasn't too hard. I was always trying to make my mom's house look nice but she kept changing everything around," he said, going through some clothes to pick out what he was going to wear to the club later that night. Then, while sorting through some clothes, he threw a bag on the table. "Do you want to break that up?"

Jason looked at the bag and saw the contents immediately. Before long the two were smoking a nice home rolled blunt with a drink at their sides. Jason wound up coughing really bad, but that is why they had the drinks by their side.

The first thing that the boys did was go out to eat, as the small amount of food they bought from the café earlier that day was completely digested. They went to a nice little Italian café and enjoyed a large plate of food along with a brilliantly green salad with freshly shredded parmesan cheese. The two boys talked a lot about each other, giving each other compliments and admiring the other. Jason admitted that he personally loved Danny's laugh, and Danny admitted he loved Jason's face when he was confused about something. The waitress was excellent, considering she was Jason's friend, Shelley. She would come over and sit next to Jason, involving herself into their conversations. Jason hoped that she wouldn't realize that he smoked, but she could probably tell.

"Stitla, Adriana, and Ron are all here," she informed him.

"Really, where?" Jason asked, turning around in his chair trying to locate them with his eyes.

"Back in the corner there," she said, pointing at the corner of the restaurant opposite the boys. Jason then had Shelley take him and Danny over to their table. Stitla and Adriana shrieked in excitement.

"Jason, oh my god! I have not seen you in forever!" Stitla said, standing up to give him a hug.

"Yeah really, my gosh...and who is this lucky young man?" Adrianna asked, standing up as well to give Jason a hug and acknowledging Danny.

"Stitla, Adriana, and Rob, this is Danny," Jason said, making a gesture towards Danny.

"His boyfriend," Danny said, reaching his hand out to shake their hands. With this comment Jason caught Danny's hazel eyes and a broad smile appeared across his face.

"Nice to meet you, man," Ron said, reaching his hand out to shake Danny's. They all chatted for a few minutes catching up on old times, but shortly had to return to their table because their food was on its way.

"Love you guys," Jason said before he left the table and he was met with a warm "Love you too" from all of them at the table.

Later that night, when they got to the club they had smiles all over their faces. The music was only a source of background noise, as Jason and Danny talked almost all night. The two were so into each other that nothing could interrupt them. Jason kept thinking that Danny was the kind of guy you could cuddle up next to, but was sensitive and strong all at the same time. The two headed out of the club so that they could talk somewhere else without all of the music. Upon reaching the car, Danny took Jason by the arm and spun him around. With the fact that Jason was stoned it sent a rush of feeling through his body that was welcomed. The look in Danny's sparkling eyes melted Jason's heart as his face grew closer to Jason's. The electricity that Jason felt in this short kiss was amazing. Danny backed up only a few inches. Jason tugged his shirt towards him and kissed him for a longer period of time. The kissing grew in intensity, and lasted longer every time.

Jason, feeling really good for once in his life, walked over to the passenger door. Upon entering the car, the kissing took back up again. They kissed all the way to town. Instead of going straight to Jason's house, they wanted to make a detour to the state park for a midnight rendezvous. They would have to stop at the gas station before they made it to this park. Jason was annoyed to see that Seth's car was parked there. Seth was inside standing at the counter, and looked at Jason as he walked in. His lip curled in anger and he walked out of the store. Tameera was working behind the counter. This had been the first time he had seen her in the longest time. "Hey! What's up?" Jason said excited.

"Nothing, how are you, Jason?" Tameera asked, coming around the counter to the front. She gave him a hug, and pulled him close. "Jason, I don't know why I never listened to you, I should have. You're so smart and you only ever tried to help me. Thank you, really," she said out of nowhere.

"Don't worry about it, Tameera, it is no big deal. Hey, you live and learn," Jason said, smiling and putting a small packet of condoms on the counter.

"Oh, in a little bit of a hurry?" Tameera said, smiling and ringing them up.

"Um, yeah, Danny is out there," Jason said, pointing over his shoulder.

"Really? But he, like, disappeared a few months ago."

"Yeah I know, I found him again found him today at the cafe."

"Wow, well have fun, oh, and call me. I live at home with my mom again!" she yelled after him as he left the store.

"Okay!" he yelled back before the door closed behind him. Jason saw that Seth's car was still there but got into his car and they quickly peeled out of the parking lot and headed up the street to the state park.

"Why was that kid looking at you all like that?" Danny asked.

"Who, Seth? He has always been an asshole." Jason fumbled for a cigarette.

"Give me one?"

"Sure...but he's gay. This one time I went to this house with this boy, I saw them making out. After that Seth really despised me. He was always acting tough, but I always knew he was a fairy," Jason said laughing.

They were cruising through a part that they always used to drive by in their smoking days. Danny had always said how beautiful this one part looked. "Okay, now park in there, kind of in the bushes," Jason said, pointing at a little lump of bushes. "Now come with me," Jason said, running around to the driver side door and pulling Danny from the car. The two began to kiss immediately. When Jason ran into the woods, Danny followed.

When the two were in a relatively sheltered area, they began to make out again and strip down to nothing. The full moon reflected off their bodies, casting silvery shadows across the woodland floor. The heat, passion, and the love that was felt in that area was enough to wake up the entire forest. Jason experienced the best hour of his life in those woods. The two began walking back to the car holding each other close, and couldn't help but to kiss. When they got to where Danny's car was, a sudden feeling of surprise and fear fell over them. "Wasn't that the car at the gas station?" Danny asked, looking over at Jason just to see him nodding his head.

With that, they heard a voice from behind them. The last thing Danny heard was a loud smack, and a thud.

Chapter 20

"So you thought you were gonna tell the world about me! You and your boyfriend, huh?" Seth yelled, before hitting Danny with the branch he had in his hand.

"Seth! Seth! Stop it!" Jason exclaimed as loud as he could through his excruciating pain. He quickly stood and ran at Seth.

"Shut up, you fuckin' faggot!" Seth said, hitting Jason with the branch. Jason was hit in his face, and pain rushed through his face. "Because of you, everyone knows!"

"Seth, I never told anybody, I never would. I understand, Seth, I can help you work through this," Jason said, trying to push himself up. With that he felt another blow to his arms, and then his back. He could hear his bones crack with each hard blow he took. "God! Why, why are you doing this to us?" Danny ran at Seth's legs, but was reflected with a blow to the side of his face. A sickening crunch was heard, and Danny lay sprawled on the forest floor.

"Shut the fuck up!" Seth screamed back. "Well, I'm sorry, Jason, but I have to get rid of you, because you outted me," Seth said, getting rope out from the back of his car. The tears were pouring from

Jason's eyes, blurring his vision. He could already feel blood trickling from his body. He looked over and saw Danny laying there motionless, and his heart sank.

"Please Seth; c'mon, I really can help you. You don't have to hurt anyone. Seth, please, pull yourself together. I won't even get you in trouble," Jason begged.

"Too late, I'm going to hell anyway!" he said, rummaging through his trunk.

"You're not going to hell just because you're gay!" Jason said, trying to think quickly. He noticed then that Danny was coming around. He motioned for him to get into the car while Seth wasn't paying attention. Danny was successful. Jason had just reached his hand up to open the door when he was knocked out cold. Seth had slammed him in the back of the head. A terrible prickling feeling worked its way to the front of his head. His head then smashed off the side of Danny's car. He lay there motionless. Seth dragged Jason over to the back of his car, and tied the rope around his legs. He had the rope attached to the hook of this trunk, and tugged on it to make sure it was strong. Danny came at him again. Though determined he was no match for the jab he received in his stomach. It sent him backward. Then a blow to the side of the head and back left him weak. Seth then quickly got into his car and started it. The starting of the engine brought Jason back to his senses.

His stomach began doing somersaults, and his limbs began to tingle as the adrenaline rushed through his veins as he struggled to get the rope off of him. Danny came running out of the car, crying and screaming, trying everything to get the rope off of Jason. Before Jason even had a chance to start burning the rope with his lighter, he felt a tug. Then he felt himself sliding across the forest floor. Danny ran along, still trying to untie the rope but it was of no use. Before long, Jason felt the asphalt against his back. He began struggling madly as the pain was ripping through him. He couldn't hear anything but the car, and his own flesh rolling off of him. The pain and agony seemed to last forever, as he tried his best to not touch the ground. After what seemed like five minutes, but was only a matter of seconds, Seth ran head on into a tree.

Jason's movement ceased and he tried to look around and figure out where he was. Nothing seemed familiar to him, and he was in a right state of shock and pain. He saw lights coming towards him but remained lying there, as he didn't want to move, or even thought he could. The car stopped close and he watched somebody get out of the car and come running towards him.

"Jason! Jason! Oh my God, Oh my God, are you okay? Oh my God," Danny said, shaking madly and looking extremely pale. Danny went into the back seat of his car, and pulled out a cover. "Jason, here, I'm gonna put this under you, and I'm gonna tie it really tight okay?" He said, lifting Jason's back and throwing the blanket under him.

"Danny," Jason said very softly, eyes wide. He scrambled back to Jason. Tears were flowing down Jason's bloody cheek.

"What?" Danny asked frantically.

"Stay by me please, please!" Jason said, allowing tears to flow down his eyes, catching his breath at the pain that was intensified by the tears.

"Okay," Danny said, looking at Jason with tears pouring from his eyes. Jason thought about a lot of things, and he suddenly remembered the lady at Atlantic City that went weird, telling him, "Have fun now, you might not get another chance." That was it; she knew this was going to happen. Tameera was that life long friend that the lady told him about. He let her go though, he let her go! He wanted to be a father; a godfather was good enough. He wanted a boyfriend, and to see the ocean, and go places and see things. He had done all of that. Then he remembered his tarot reading, having a bad future, but only for a short time. He had accomplished his goal of trusting people more and standing up for himself, rather than allowing everyone to walk all over him. He then began thinking of things he hadn't done, being a scientist, a successful wealthy man. With all of these thoughts coming and going, Jason began to cry. He also knew that this was it; it was time for him to go. No matter what anyone else said, he was going home today to a place beyond the planes of this earth. He then really felt the life he had left trying to leave his body. He was then struck with fear, fear of what may happen next. He turned to Danny, "Danny! Danny! I'm dying."

"Oh God no! No, don't say that. Jason, hang in there!" Danny cried. He could see all the blood that was lost. The asphalt had rubbed its way straight to the bone in some places. There was a particularly nasty blood stream coming from his left leg.

"I can't, it's not that easy, but listen…" Jason said, feeling a depressed, sad, giving up feeling, "…I love you, tell my family I love them, oh God!" He screamed out painfully, knowing he was only seconds away from letting go. Jason had to concentrate as hard as he could to hold on as long as he could. "Bye."

"Jason, no! Hold on, hang in there." Danny demanded, tears dropping rapidly off of his cheeks. "I love you!" he said, giving Jason a kiss on the cheek. "Here they come, Jason; here comes the ambulance, just hold on," Danny said, looking down at him.

"Danny…I love you with all my heart." He cried, like no one could every cry. "I love you," Jason stated just before he could hold onto life no longer. Danny watched as his body went limp and his eyes closed.

"Oh my God! Jason, no! Please, no! Oh my God! Jason!" Danny screamed, holding Jason in his arms. Danny was shaking vigorously, now traumatized as he was now holding a dead body in his arms. It wasn't just any dead body. It was the body of the man he loved, of the one he had selfishly declined several times before, and now when he was finally ready to open his arms to him, he was gone. He didn't want to let go and bent over Jason crying.

"Son, let go of him," the EMT said to Danny, hurriedly bending over Jason and checking for vital signs. "He has no vital signs, call in the medevac," the EMT shouted backwards, then in a hushed voice said, "Oh my God, Jason, what happened to you." Randy, the EMT, couldn't believe what he was seeing. Jason now lay dead in a pool of his own blood. It left the blanket soaked in blood. Despite this scene, the whole team quickly began to try and resuscitate him.

Danny sat back and watched and just cried and cried, hoping that in some way Jason's soul would come back into his body. He didn't want this great thing to be over. He loved Jason and could not live on without him. This day was perfect, it was everything Danny had ever dreamed of, and now the one that he loved was gone. Jason did not realize all the times that Danny sat up and thought of Jason. He was young, so he could not get in touch with him. He probably sat awake at night thinking about Jason as much as Jason had himself of Danny. Now, however, that was gone. No more Jason. Danny himself soon blacked out from blood loss and the overwhelming pain, not just physical, but emotional as well.

Chapter 21

Jason's mother was at home waiting up for Terrance when she received a knock on the door. Her face fell as she heard the news that the sheriff had to tell her. She began crying and fell to the floor, wailing in pure agony. Her face red with pain, his siblings began to wake up and come down. They asked their mother what was wrong. She told them that their brother was dead. Melissa did not want to believe it and looked out the door, but before long she too began crying, asking where he was. Kyle just sat down on the stairs and stared at the wall and began to cry, with large giant tears falling down his face. Ashley, Jason's other little sister, helped her mother up and then hugged her there on the floor and they just cried into each other's shoulders.

The sheriff just stood there with his hat off and head down in respect to the family of this boy who had just died a horrific death. He stood there and answered any questions that they had.

"How did he die?" his mother asked.

"He was beaten with a blunt object and dragged behind the back of a car," the sheriff responded in deep regret that he had to give this information to this poor family. "He bled to death."

"How long ago did he die?" Melissa asked, looking up with tears still filling her eyes.

"He was pronounced dead at twelve-thirty-five this morning."

"Where is he now?" Jason's mother asked, attempting to stand up.

"He was taken to the morgue at the hospital," the sheriff said, "We do need you to come down to the hospital to sign an official form stating that you know that he is your son, Jason Lizanich."

"Okay, will you lead the way?" his mother asked.

"I would be more than happy to do that for you, ma'am," the sheriff said, "whenever you're ready."

The scene at the morgue when they arrived was a pitiful sight. Only Jason's mother was allowed to enter to identify the body, and when she came out of the room she was crying frantically. She now had all the proof that she needed. Her son, whom she loved so much and would die for, was now lying dead in the room next door.

It wasn't long before news crews from all over the place made their way up to this back country road to report on what had happened. The amount of people that Jason had touched through his life was amazing, as more and more people came to pay their respects to him. People were coming from all the way across the country, as word got out that Jason was gay and was killed because of it.

The public was still trying to sort out this act of violence in their minds. They couldn't understand why one guy who was just like the other one would kill him. It made no sense to most of the American public. The people that listened to Danny came closer to any type of understanding.

Seth was reported dead at the scene, but he did not get as much attention as Jason had. His family was rattled and his dad flipped out when he found out that Seth was a homosexual. No one really understood why Jason had to die at such a young age because of the way he was.

Upon the death of Jason, a revolution was in the making. People all rallied to try and educate the public about homosexuality. The church mourned, but also found a way to make a mockery of the situation, stating that a life of sin will lead to an untimely death.

Jason's mother also felt more dread than a lot of people, as she realized that she should have spent more quality time getting to know her son, rather than criticizing his lifestyle. Danny had broken down completely and moved out on his own to a different area far away from this small town. Everywhere he looked he was reminded of Jason. He had been sorry that they only got to spend such a short amount of time together in the last couple of years, but he did love Jason.

Danny was sick of people treating him like he was a celebrity. He would take that media attention and try to get people to see the real picture. They were always adding him onto statistics and so on and so forth.

Danny could not bring himself to even think of dating other people, and even the people in his new town knew who he was. He knew that he had to get a move on in his own life, but he could not get Jason out of his mind ever. It was because of this that made today an important day for Danny.

The deep dark place had crept up on him very quickly. There were times that Danny was sure Jason would do things that would let him know he was there. When Danny moved he decorated in very much the same way, including the exquisite decoration of candles and sea shells. Every once in a while he would come home and a sea shell would be out of place or a candle moved closer to the other candles. Danny thought of these things a lot. Then he remembered talking at the restaurant, and he remembered all the times that Jason looked confused.

Danny began to laugh, but then began to cry, feeling that tear in his heart rip open once more with thoughts of Jason. Today, he put the gun to his head. He loved Jason and no one else. He had nothing anymore. He hadn't eaten in two weeks, and lost all drive and motivation. He knew there was nothing he could do. He was supposed to die too. He told Jason he was coming. He let out a small laugh with his thoughts of Jason.

Danny looked at the picture he had of Jason. The tears literally began pouring out of his eyes. He kissed the picture, and felt his heart yearn to be with Jason. There was now nothing more to think on.

"Jason, I love you." He then pulled the trigger.

Printed in the United States
64790LVS00003B/179